Dewdrops

Dewdrops

SONA BALSAM

PARTRIDGE

To order additional copies of this book, contact
Partridge India
000 800 10062 62
orders.india@partridgepublishing.com

www.partridgepublishing.com/india

"In three words I can sum up everything I have learned about life... 'It goes on!'"

-Robert Frost

To my little sunshine Arjun.
To my parents and my sister.
And to everyone who stood by me 'Always'!

Acknowledgement

Thanks to Madam Selvi, my English teacher for her constant encouragement on every attempt that I made in writing during my school days.

Thanks to Dad who read my manuscript first.

Thanks to my friend Nirmal Ram who gave me an unbiased honest review.

And thanks a lot Uncle Selva and Uncle Muruganandam for your reviews and blessings.

A very special thanks to my friend Ramshanker, who took some time out of his busy music schedule to compose the Author Note.

I'd like to thank Antoniet Saints, Author Advisor from Partridge Publishing House, Bloomington.

Also Jake Rivers and Racel Cruz, Senior Publishing Consultants from Partridge Publishing House, Bloomington.

I'd like to extend my gratitude to Pohar Baruah, Publishing Services Associate from Partridge Publishing House, Bloomington.

Thanks to everyone who played a part in the making over of my manuscript into a published book.

Prologue

March, the beginning of Summer - the season of sun has come along with its warmth. The season of summer has its own beauty in announcing its arrival – the beautiful, red Gulmohur flowers with its own eye catching charm and the golden leaves and the beautiful birds singing along the welcome note not to mention the scorching heat and the heat waves. To crown it all... the exams. Most of us prefer the other side of the exams which means the vacation.

In this season, the roads bordered with trees on both sides are strewn with golden leaves. The park benches beneath the trees sheltered in the shadow of the trees feels just like heaven. And sitting inside the college bus gives you an experience on how exactly a turkey feels when inside the microwave oven.

Now let me tell you about Chennai and its summer. When you wake up in the morning from your bed, you'll be actually wondering whether you are out of a swimming pool. Even at seven in the morning it gets sunny. As you walk along an empty street in the morning, you'll feel as if you are a part of some landscape painting because everything around you will be so static. Not even a single leaf will move. You cannot survive without an air conditioner but the unfortunate thing is as you step out of your comfortable air conditioned room into the real weather you'll be actually thinking whether you have been kidnapped over to the Sahara. At times, you'll feel like stepping into some air conditioned shops just to avoid the sun. Sounds ridiculous?

But I definitely appreciate the will power and the tolerance of the lovers who adorn the beaches every single day. Come whatever may, be it the scorching heat or the tsunami, they are never deterred.

Like every other place on Earth, Chennai also has got its unique flavor and having lived in this city for about four years I've fallen in love with it. Something keeps happening here. Chennai is very special in its own way.

Well…. I don't wanna write a travelogue about this full of life, active, electrifying and bubbly city now. Coming to the point, I just wanted to say that I'm gonna be back in this city and I have missed it so much in the past few months.

Chapter 1

Could it be just a dream? It was pitch dark… as if a black cloth had been tied across to cover my eyes. I know I've been unconscious for a long time. But… How long? I don't know. Maybe hours… or even days on end.

I must've been dead long before. Oh! Then is this what death is? But this can't be death. Or could it be? Who knows? No one who has ever gone to the doors of death has returned back to tell his tales. It can only happen to super heroes and I am no super human for that matter.

I'm thinking and that exactly is the problem with me. Have you ever heard of a person with thinking problem? You will get used to it as soon as you come to know me better. I do think a lot for an average girl… more than necessary. My imagination is my worst enemy. I should be kept in a museum for having escaped the hands of death himself.

Though I have kept my eyes closed, the memory that had last registered in my mind keep flashing in front of my eyes.

I clearly remember the Wedding reception party, the balcony of the hotel from where I slipped or (jumped, but I haven't got enough nerves to jump from such an altitude and so that could never have happened) or imagined that I slipped for I felt someone brushing against me as I was trying to have a look at someone who I never wish to see again in my life if I ever survive. Priya was standing right beside me when I fell. I don't remember where Preethi was but I saw Sid's shocked face before I fell. I've always wanted a sweet brother like Sid; at least he is a great friend of mine! But I am really confused as usual… how did I ever manage to look at my friends even at the peak tension when my life was dangling by almost a thread? But I don't remember hitting the floor. I just kept on falling like Alice did when she fell into the rabbit hole and after that everything is a blank. Maybe I passed out or else I should have been dead before even hitting the floor. Poor heart of mine! But there is no necessity for me to be dead because I have been roaming around as a living dead for the past two years.

But why would Priya want to kill me. I never meant any harm to her. She can hardly want revenge. She never got to know me even.

I have been trying to open my eyes in spite of my heavy eyelids for a long time with barely any success. From what I feel I can say that I'm lying on a bed like a log for ages. No matter how much effort I put to wake up I couldn't move a muscle.

After a long struggle, I open my eyes very slowly to find myself in some kind of a dark room. I've never been here before. As my eyes began to adjust to the darkness, I found out that the curtains were drawn so secure that not even a single ray of light could enter the room. So I couldn't find out what time it is… whether day or night; dawn or dusk; twilight or noon. How long have I been here? This definitely is not a place for normal people.

Talking about NORMAL- You could never relate me to the word 'normal'. I am of the opinion that a normal person doesn't fall in love or even from a balcony for that matter.

A normal person is never the target of Cupid's arrow. And here in my case it was I who went resolutely in front of Cupid so that I could be his target rather than anyone else.

I should have expected to find myself in such a strange place after having been about to be murdered or let's call it an unpleasant accident because I hate murders and policemen and all those long investigations on conspiracy that follows as well. I am lying on a bed with clean white sheets, the color which has always made me go crazy but not now. To my left are certain medical gadgets which everyone would have seen in the climax of most Indian movies where someone was about to die, mostly heroes did, giving young girls of my age a heart ache.

Suddenly the fact hit me hard.

'Oh my God!' I wondered.

I looked across the gloomy room. Only one place on this planet could look like this and I don't want to be there. Now that my eyes have adjusted to the darkness around me I could make out the letters I.C.U written in reverse written on a hard glass door. I never imagined even in my worst dreams that I would end up in an I.C.U. I hate being a patient in hospitals because it reminded me of my school day failures. My parents had always had great hopes pinned upon me that I would become a great doctor but I ended up being an engineer. My mom even today can't take that fact easy though I am well settled now.

She used to tell me that she had imagined me as a doctor even when I was in her womb. Well… These sentimental family dialogues are always a bit too much for me to bear which would often send me fast to my room with the door banging behind me with as much force that could produce the loudest noise that would definitely make my mum glare at me with anger. But I never cared. My prime motto of irritating her by expressing my fury will be achieved this way.

Once upon a time, my life was like… I was lucky all the time. I was always happy. To crown it all, everyone seemed to love me a lot. But now whenever I begin to think that everything is going to be ok, it definitely is not.

A slow creak.

The door of my room opened slowly.

'Who is that?' I thought.

My head began to spin and my heart almost missed a beat when I recognized the person- the most handsome guy, a girl can ever find in this universe. My knight in armour has come to see his damsel in distress. The person whom I least wanted to meet… at least at this juncture… entered the room. I didn't want him to see me in this distasteful situation. But the other half of my mind was silently rejoicing the moment of his comeback. His face was pale and expressionless as he neared me. I felt the broken pieces of my heart breaking into dust as I realized he was sad. This proved that I'm leaving him alone at last… I am gonna die soon and that is what I need at this moment, a rapid end rather than living a hell of a life where my love has left me alone to suffer in the wilderness. His sorrow was visible in his eyes. It hurt him a lot to see me like this and that exactly is what I wanted. I wanted to hurt him. I wanted to yell at him and hit him. But that would hurt me too. After all that he had done to me why should I have any feelings for him? But I still do have. And this proves I am mad. Completely insane. He knelt beside me and held my hand in his and whispered the same words he once told me when I was suffering from something as normal as cold, "You'll be fine". The only difference is that at that time he was telling me the truth.

'No Aditya… I am leaving you finally. You have no obstacles or mood spoilers in your life anymore' I whispered.

Then all of a sudden…

A blinding light flashed to my left and something began to scream. A horrible scream. And my bed began to vibrate. He got up and there was a cacophony of noise and the room was in an absolute pandemonium as people began rushing in. I tried to move but something was pushing me back. And things started to dissolve around me until everything was blank. All I knew was that he was holding my hand and that was enough for me to die happily. Yes, true to his words he had stood by me forever holding my hands and never let go of me. The noise grew louder and louder… until Sarah woke up.

Sarah woke up with a start.

*****

Chapter 2

'What the hell?' thought Sarah as she opened her eyes and tried to recollect her dream. Her new cell phone which she had ultimately decided to buy, she had bought herself a brand new iphone and abandoned her old cell phone (which she had possessed during her college days and called as croaky affectionately and without which she couldn't imagine even one day in her life and that usually lay by her bedside) was screaming and the display flashed 'Preethi'.

'Why the hell would she call at this unearthly hour?' thought Sarah.

Of course the room was dark and the curtains were drawn together. It was pitch black except for the flash of the cell phone. It must be around midnight.

Sarah's eyes started to adjust to the darkness as she pressed the speak icon of the phone.

'Hello', Sarah said in a sleepy voice as she switched on the table lamp.

'Wake up Sarah! You wanted me to wake you up at four', Preethi's voice came from the other end.

'Is it four already?' asked Sarah fumbling with the alarm clock on the table and added 'I thought it was midnight. Thanks Preethi. I will be up in a minute. But…Should I really come Preethi?' asked Sarah in a half sleepy voice.

'If you are gonna start that row again I'll never talk to you Sarah. Get up and you are supposed to be at my home for lunch' replied Preethi and disconnected the call.

Sarah cursed under her breath and sat still on her bed trying to recollect what she had seen in her dream. The more she tried to remember the more she forgot and she was definitely thankful to her memory for that. She didn't want to remember all those terrible nightmares. 'There was definitely a dark room. And someone walked in… then what happened? Er… The cell phone screamed' thought Sarah and convinced herself. Finally she got tired of trying to remember the dream and got up from her bed after about ten minutes. She felt the chillness creep up through her spine as she placed her legs on the floor since it was winter.

Sarah and Preethi are supposed to attend their friend Vinitha's wedding that was about to take place in Chennai the next week. Sarah was well known in Preethi's family and Preethi's mom was very fond of Sarah. Preethi and Sarah had been best friends throughout college. She was treated almost as one among their family.

Sarah had secured a scholarship to do her MS in a reputed University in USA and an internship with 'Facebook', her dream and she was leaving to the United States in the next two months. She had been on a lonely tour to North India- Delhi and some nearby hill stations for the past two weeks. She was currently staying in her cousin's home in Delhi. She had been totally stressed out for all that she had undergone in her college days. So she had taken a break now. If there was ever one fact that she regretted in her life, it was that she had fallen so madly in love with a guy in her college days. As a result she had stopped watching romantic movies and reading such novels and she lost faith in love because that relationship had ended in such a way she had never imagined. May be she was also a reason for the end... as well as the beginning.

Sarah left the house by six after bidding a round of goodbye to her cousin's family. Her cousin's husband offered to drive her to the airport but she refused saying that she had some work on the way. So the driver was sent to drop her and she was enjoying every second of her journey by car. She loved travelling a lot but now she had developed a special liking for this place over the days of her stay that she found it difficult to leave. She told herself that she would come back again as soon as possible. Cool breeze was blowing upon her face and it refreshed her. They reached the airport in half an hour and she sent the driver back immediately. She preferred being alone these days.

As she was walking on the pavement leading to the Airport she noticed the dewdrops that had settled themselves cozily in the leaf blades of the grass in the sidewalk of the airport lane shone like diamonds in the sunlight. Sarah was staring at the sparkling beauty of the dewdrops as she walked. And the sun began to shine brighter, the dew melted and rolled on the leaf blade and finally it was gone leaving behind its freshness on the greenery. How similar nature's phenomenon is to human behavior! The teardrops that roll down our eyes after getting hurt by the one we love almost drains us out of feelings and emotions when they finally disappear leaving us with a new beginning, a fresh start.

Her flight to Chennai was scheduled at half past eight. She bought herself a sandwich and was sitting in the lounge going through the day's newspaper. When she was browsing the daily magazine she came across a tidbit that her favourite singer Enrique Iglesias has a plan to visit India. Music…How much had she been mad about music earlier? She had been a great fan of Enrique and Taylor Swift. This news kindled the past memories of her first year in college.

*****

The college cultural fest was in full swing. It was Sarah's first year in that engineering college where people who had lacked luck in their twelfth grade studied. Most of the first years were irritated by their seniors' stupid behavior as they expected their seniors to behave at least to some extent, decent.

As for Sarah, becoming an engineer is the last thing on earth she ever wished. She had always had this passion for animation, movies, fashion and literature. She enjoyed writing articles for magazines. She was a fun loving girl but she was a hard worker too. She had always been a top scorer in school, teachers' pet and undoubtedly popular. Her parents who are doctors themselves had wanted her to become a doctor like every parent who craves for a doctor heir in their family. Unfortunately her score had gone down to an all time low in her school leaving examination. Now that she had ended up in a stupid engineering college due to her fate which she had begun to hate from the day she had secured an admission there, she was furious with her mum who had suggested her to pursue a career in engineering now that she had no hope of getting into medicine.

Coming back to the cultural events, whenever a department other than the all time famous Mechanical department scored a point higher, there began the famous chair fight. Most of you would have heard of a sword fight but definitely not a chair fight. It is the unique fight of most engineering colleges in Chennai which had taken many a juniors by awe and wonder. Then the members from the Disciplinary committee would be sent to bring the situation under control. The guys from the Mechanical department sported a black T-shirt with the caption 'No Girls, No Love, No problem'. For every cheer of the other department students, the Mech guys booed and made faces. Sarah had made friends with Preethi and Vinitha both from the department of IT. Vinitha and Preethi were roommates. It was their third week into college and they have already begun to miss their school days so badly that they were even ready to face the horrible Board Exams once again rather than staying in this hell of a college.

Sarah, Preethi and Vinitha returned from the canteen to the auditorium after a hearty lunch to see what event was going on the stage. They decided to settle down in the chairs arranged middle way from the stage hidden behind a group of third year CSE girls. They tried to keep as far away from the Mech guys as possible because they didn't want to get caught in the midst of their chair fight or their crazy off stage dance. The Group singing event had begun and they had never in their life witnessed such a boring event. Preethi almost fell down asleep. If it hadn't been for Vinitha she would have fallen straight to the floor and hit her nose. Sarah pretended to be watching the program while sleeping with her eyes open the same way she does during her boring class lectures.

To their greatest relief, the last group was announced,

'Finally we have Aditya and Siddharth's band of third year ECE on stage'.

Sarah looked up as every girl in the crowd was cheering so loudly that even Preethi had woken up with a start.

Sarah watched the two guys on the stage accompanied by two other guys. Aditya and Siddharth seemed fairly familiar to her.

Then as soon as she recognized them…

'Hey Preethi! Look! It's those guys!' exclaimed Sarah.

'What guys?' asked Preethi her tone quite smug as her sleep had been interrupted.

'I told you a week ago.'

'Well... You've told me about a million guys. Which one is this supposed to mean?'

'The guys who called me Miss. Smile that day' replied Sarah with a smile.

'Very well! But stop blushing now, will you?' said Preethi in a teasing tone.

'I am not blushing!' Sarah angrily retorted and her smile suddenly vanished.

'They are handsome of course. Anyway Sarah, Good choice! But which one is yours?'

Sarah gave Preethi a glare which made Preethi go suddenly quiet.

The guy Aditya, tall (5' 10" – So isn't that tall?) and ruggedly handsome with an athletic build was a guitarist and a lead singer too. His hair had been done pretty well using gel but Sarah was not good enough to know what style it was but it definitely looked good on him. His eyes were so sharp that it mesmerized Sarah, so she looked away whenever she thought their eyes met. Sid who was an inch or two taller than Aditya and had a goatee was a brilliant drummer. If Sid was smart then Aditya was smarter. Both of them were very good friends and people often mistook them for twins. In Sarah's words- Both were good looking, smart and well groomed gentlemen with a good dressing sense. The other two guys, one was a keyboard player and the other a guitarist too. Sarah didn't know their names but she had her eyes only for Aditya.

At least this college had two decent looking lads with a good dressing sense in Sarah's opinion-Aditya and Siddharth.

When the guys started with their song, Sarah exclaimed, 'Oh My God! Preethi! Doesn't he sing like Enrique?' She had said it a bit louder than she had expected to sound for all the senior girls around her frowned at her. Some said 'Shh'.

'Oops! I'm sorry' she apologized and muttered under her breath to Preethi 'Why don't they mind their own businesses?'

'If only they had any…' was Preethi's reply.

Aditya and Sid's band was halfway through the song Nickel back's 'Far away'. Sarah was a diehard fan of the singer Enrique Iglesias. Though the song was different, Aditya's voice left her awestruck… it was very much like Enrique's. And though both the guys were equally handsome, there was something in Aditya that made him stand apart. She was not sure whether it was his eyes or the voice that left her in a half dreamy state. Moreover Aditya was wearing a white shirt with blue jeans which according to Sarah was the best attire in the world that could make any girl to turn her head to have a look at any guy.

Just as the song got over, there was a thunderous applause from the girls that made even the Mech guys to sit quiet.

'Preethi! I simply love that guy… Aditya' Sarah exclaimed.

'Oh really Sarah?' laughed Preethi.

For the first time Sarah noticed a girl with long hair sitting right in front of Preethi. She turned and looked at Sarah. Her eyes expressed a suppressed anger. Sarah didn't know what to say. She simply smiled which made the girl turn her back to Sarah.

Sarah was puzzled. She whispered to Preethi 'Who is she?'

'She is a third year. Some Priya from your crazy department. Must be a mad fan of Aditya like you who is ready to stand in a queue carrying a placard or something of the sort you would like to carry saying 'Marry me Aditya' and blah blah blah'.

'Stop it, will you? Or I will make you regret what you just said' retorted Sarah.

Preethi stopped commenting because she knew very well that Sarah was capable of doing what she said.

Before the cultural fest had begun, a week ago, a few seniors from the event organization board had gone to the junior classrooms to invite the first years to participate in the events. Two very smart guys whom Sarah did not know at that time entered her class.

They were none other than Aditya and Siddharth.

Sid announced 'Hello First years! Welcome to our college! Hope you are having fun!'

For this the entire class booed.

He continued 'Oops! Got fed up already? So… That's the reason why we have come to announce the cultural fest that's gonna take place in our college in the next couple of days and I want every one of you to participate…' And he went on about the list of events that will take place and the guests who were about to come and blah blah blah.

'As if they had invited Spielberg as chief guest…' whispered Sarah to her bench mate Maya and they both were giggling about something and talking some girly girly stuff throughout Sid's soliloquy.

Sid called out, 'Oy Miss Smile! I will announce a smiling contest if you wish to join. You wanna join?'

Sarah immediately said 'No!' and nodded fast.

'Then be quiet Missy' said Sid and the girls started laughing on seeing the look on Sarah's face. Actually every girl in the class knew Sid before (but he didn't know them) because Sid was one of the Mr. Popular in the college and they were ready to giggle for anything he said. But if you think this made Sarah to stop giggling you are mistaken. She kept giggling with the others.

At last they asked the students to maintain discipline and decorum during the event. Before leaving the class, Aditya said 'And one more thing… Giggling girls are gonna get into trouble sooner or later' and pointed to Sarah. This was more of a comment rather than a warning.

Sarah actually began to admire their attitude. She somehow knew she would be friends with them soon. But every time she followed them to start a conversation she ended up meeting a bunch of Aditya and Sid's class girls who frowned at her or nodded disapprovingly at her. She even got told off by them twice for talking a bit too louder. She got too scared to continue and so she stopped stalking them but did not forget to smile at them whenever she crossed them.

'I don't understand why smiling is taken as an offence over here' remarked Sarah to Preethi.

'Because we only do that dear' replied Preethi.

*****

Chapter 3

The flight to Chennai took off. Sarah looked around her once again in search of any familiar faces but no luck. The woman sitting near her was busy reading a book… some middle age novel in which Sarah had no interest. And obviously, the woman too was least interested in conversation. So Sarah didn't want to disturb her either. She left her alone with her book.

Past memories were flooding once again into her mind like the woolly clouds outside the window. She didn't want to get carried away once again. So she decided to shoo them away. No success. She took her magazine from her bag and started to read it. She came across the article 'Most haunted shopping malls…'

That was it. She couldn't stop the memories unfurling in front of her eyes.

*****

The day was quite bright and it was the usual weather condition in Chennai. Well… You can't expect a snowfall over there. So shopping in an air conditioned mall will be considered heavenly by anyone who had traveled almost an hour by bus to reach there. This was the first time Sarah had come out with her friends Preethi and Vinitha to the oldest famous hang around spot for almost all the college students as well as the window shoppers in the past decade - 'Spencer Plaza'.

In hostel, Vinitha could not be found with the other two. She will prefer to remain shut in her room alone with her cell phone as company. She had a boy friend who spent hundreds on her phone bills. Preethi and Sarah hated the idea of having a boyfriend after seeing Vinitha and her cell phone. Sarah had nicknamed that cell phone as '24 x 7'.

After about two hours of mall walk (window shopping is the exact term) during which Vinitha's cell phone rang at least four times, the three of them settled down in a cozy corner in the food court which according to Preethi was the best place in all the malls. As soon as they found chairs and sat down Vinitha became busy with her 24 x 7.

'Sick!' said Sarah on seeing her and rolled her eyes.

'Anything for love' replied Preethi in a sarcastic tone and the two of them giggled.

'I've heard love is blind but she's gonna be deaf soon with all those phone calls' said Sarah.

Vinitha took the least notice of them. She always ignored their comments. Though Preethi and Vinitha were roommates Preethi spent most of her time in

Sarah's room. Preethi's Mom and brother lived in Chennai and so she went home most weekends and Sarah tagged along. She stayed in hostel only to avoid traveling every day.

The food court was dimly lit and it looked inviting. The windows had red drapes hung over them. The place looked like a pretty little China town. The aroma of burgers mixed with that of the pastries was in the air that kindled their hunger.

'This is called "Love is in the air" I reckon. What do you say Sarah?' asked Preethi.

'Maybe' replied Sarah looking around.

Round the corner, they sold popcorn; sweet corn boiled and grilled with butter; ice creams of different flavors and chaat items.

'Who wants popcorn? I'll get one' said Sarah and started towards that corner.

She bought a big cone full of popcorn and was paying for it when a big red balloon flew past her. She tried to catch it but it was too fast to her reflexes. It was a gracious one in its flight. She took a last glance at the balloon and was thinking to herself 'Did I just call that balloon gracious? I must be mad calling a balloon…' and turned round the corner when someone banged straight into her.

'Ouch' she screamed.

Her popcorn flew up into the air and spilled all over her. She looked up to see who had caused such mayhem. She couldn't believe her eyes… her eyes had found the guy from whom she couldn't take her eyes off…Aditya. She stood dumbstruck and her heart had started singing her favourite tunes. She had thought about him in the morning when she was in the bus. And now he was right there in front of her very eyes.

'I'm sorry. I was after that balloon' apologized Aditya and went in the direction of the red balloon which now lay near the corner of the pop corn stall.

Preethi was hiding her laugh when Sarah returned back to the table with her face a tiny shade of pink. Vinitha, who had no idea of what had happened as she was sitting with her back to the view, finally switched off her 24 x 7 and said 'There is popcorn in your hair Sarah. And you look funny.'

'Know how it happened? Aditya banged on me and spilled popcorn all over me' said Sarah with her eyes full of amusement.

'I witnessed that amazing scene. Our sweetheart Sarah was standing like a statue trying to get the words out of her mouth but... did you manage to reply at all honey?' said Preethi in a teasing tone and added 'So we go without popcorn.'

'Well... I'll get us something else then' said Vinitha and walked towards the 'Marry Brown' shop counter.

As soon as Vinitha left, another surprising scene awaited Sarah again. Aditya appeared in front of her with a big cone of popcorn. To his left was a girl with long hair who looked so familiar. 'Priya who frowned at me during the cultural fest' thought Sarah. Sarah and Preethi exchanged a quick glance at each other for a moment as the two approached their table. Priya was about Preethi's height. She was in a bright yellow salwar and looked like a sunflower. Her hair was tied in a long plait. She looked glum as if she had long forgotten how to smile. In her hands was that red balloon that she held in a way as if it was not her wish to hold it.

'A typical senior' thought Preethi but dared not to voice it.

'So you caught the balloon finally?' Sarah enquired Aditya with a smile.

'I'm really sorry. I wasn't looking properly' apologized Aditya and handed over the popcorn to her.

'Thanks!' said Sarah and added 'Well… We have met before. I'm from your college.'

'I thought you looked quite familiar. Which department?'

'The Psycho department' said Sarah and added hastily as Aditya looked puzzled 'Department of Computer Science and Engineering.'

'Oh! I remember you. Even she's from your so called psycho department' said Aditya indicating the girl to his left and added 'She's Priya'.

'You are Sarah, aren't you?' asked Priya with a tiny smile. She looked pretty when she smiled.

'Yes. I'm Sarah and this is my friend Preethi.'

They shook hands.

'Why don't you join us for lunch?' asked Sarah.

'No, thanks Sarah. Anyway it was nice meeting you all. We got to go now. See you guys later' smiled Aditya and went away with Priya. His smile was enchanting. Even Preethi agreed with Sarah on this fact. Both the girls had a topic to discuss for the rest of the day.

The two girls watched them till they disappeared round the corner. After that Sarah looked down at the popcorn and heaved a sigh.

'So Sarah…Love failure' teased Preethi.

'Oh Shut up Preethi! It's not love. I just like him' replied Sarah.

'Hypocrite!' muttered Preethi.

Before Sarah could react again Vinitha arrived with burgers and Pepsi. The idea of having lunch turned everything else out of their mind. Preethi began to eat like a wolf that had been starved for weeks on end.

'Oh my God! Preethi, you eat like a pig!' exclaimed Sarah.

'I don't care how I look when I eat' replied Preethi and continued wolfing on the food. So it was Sarah's chance to narrate what happened after Vinitha had gone to get them food. Sarah is well known to narrate tales in the way she wanted things to have taken place and with Preethi deeply involved in eating Vinitha never knew whether she was listening to the original version of the incident at all.

'So… Priya is Aditya's girlfriend?' asked Vinitha finally.

'I reckon so' replied Sarah in a tiny voice playing thoughtfully with the tomato sauce on her plate.

'Bad choice though. Is he blind?' said Preethi whose voice was muffled by the mouthful of burger.

And they went on with their girly talks about why Priya did not deserve Aditya.

'And I don't really understand why you like him Sarah. Rich show off guys – not your type, are they?' asked Vinitha.

'I dunno. I fancy his attitude. Moreover he's not a show off. And maybe it's because I find him distinct in the crowd. Anyway our college sucks big time', replied Sarah.

In the adjacent coffee shop, that was almost half empty sat Aditya and Priya in an uncomfortable silence sipping their coffee.

'What's wrong with you Priya? You keep ignoring me all these days. If I had ever done something wrong, please forgive me' pleaded Aditya to Priya earnestly.

'I am fine Aditya' snapped Priya.

'No. You are not. If anything is bothering you, you can tell me. I care for you and you know that very well.'

'Why do you still love me Aditya even after I hurt you so badly?'

'I can't give you reasons Priya. All that I know is I love you.'

'Well… Aditya! I don't want to hurt you again but the thing is… I came out with you today to tell you that this is the last time we are seeing each other.'

'What?' shouted Aditya. He was shocked. 'Stop joking Priya.'

But he knew she was not joking from the looks of it. He had feared a break up for the past one month.

'I am getting married Aditya!' announced Priya.

'What?'

'Dad and Mum said yes.'

'But you are still in college' replied Aditya.

'Actually the marriage is scheduled next year. I'm getting engaged to him next month.'

'Are you being forced into this marriage by your parents?' asked Aditya.

'No…not at all. Actually they asked my opinion. I gave a thought about it and said yes' said Priya flatly.

'But what about me? What about us? We love each other' asked Aditya earnestly.

'Well… Not anymore. Don't you see? I don't love you anymore. I have learnt to move on. I have often told you I hate you flirting with other girls.'

'Don't be silly Priya!'

'It occurred to me so fast. When my parents came out with this topic of marriage I told them about you. Of course they were furious with me but then they made me see some sense. I took some time to think over it. I just want to be practical. My fiancé works in London. After my course completion I'll go to London too. You'll still be pursuing higher studies and all that. I hope you understand…'

The word fiancé burnt through Aditya like venom.

'Priya, please. How could you be so cold?'

'Now you listen to me. You wanted to play that silly basketball match even though it meant that you can't meet me for about a month. And you hang around with that stupid guy Sid who imagines himself cool and you guys just enjoy showing off to impress girls especially the juniors. And you want to make friends with a first year who keeps hero worshipping you. And you flirt with girls saying that it makes them happy. And to crown it all you expect me to understand you? No Aditya. It's high time we stop pretending that we love each other'

'Please Priya! Don't be so childish! Why are you behaving so immature? I don't even know that first year girl we met. Sid and I just teased her once before the cultural fest. You have been with me for the past six months but you don't seem to trust me. You still keep bossing me about with whom I should be friends. Trust me Priya. I love you and I don't want to lose you at any cost. And I am not pretending Priya. I really love you' pleaded Aditya.

'Now you begin shouting at me. If you feel I am bossing you around then you should just go ahead and lead your life in your own way. Why do you want me? Just go ahead with your life Aditya. It's all over between us.'

'You are just angry. Relax now. You'll be fine soon. We will talk about this later' said Aditya in a soothing voice.

'Sorry Aditya! I have made my decision. This is it. I am not reconsidering my decisions. I am sure that we are not made for each other. I'm tired of trying to keep our relationship intact. Let's call it a break.'

She got up and moved towards the door her bag swinging in her hand. Aditya followed her fast and gripped her hand in the gentlest way a guy can and said 'Priya! Listen to me once.'

Exactly at the same moment Sarah, Preethi and Vinitha came round the corner and looked at them. By the looks of it, they understood that it was an uncomfortable situation in which they had caught Aditya and Priya and walked away silently as if they had not noticed them standing in front of them, without giving them another look but they couldn't help but hear the last few words of Priya.

Priya glared at him and released her hand from Aditya's grip and said, 'Please leave me alone Aditya. Don't mess up my already half spoilt life. Let me live it in peace' and without a backward glance at him she walked straight out of his life for the last time.

*****

Chapter 4

Aditya stood there on the second floor of the mall like a frozen statue looking at the trailing figure of Priya. For the first time in six months he had felt that Priya was serious this time. He had a feeling that she will never come back for him. Now that she had gone telling him she's getting married to someone else, the reality that she had no love for him anymore hit him badly. The feeling of being unwanted killed him.

Priya had been his girlfriend for the past one year. Once she had entered his life he had never even in his worst dreams imagined a life without her. But he always dreaded she would leave him someday. So he did whatever she asked for. It was love at first sight for them. (So they said.) But Aditya had never been able to predict her. He had often had the doubt whether she loved him at all. The more he tried to hold on to her the more she moved away from him. Try holding a handful of sand tightly in your hands; it will be fast in slipping away from your grasp.

Aditya and Priya had been friends in the social networking site 'Orkut' (It was the golden age of Orkut then before Facebook entered the arena and took over) even before college. And when they met accidentally, it seems that cupid had hit them. Priya was a silent girl and she did not have much friends. She didn't put efforts to socialize with her classmates too because she hated them. She was a kind of person who honestly believed that she was the only person on earth who was correct all the time. Sid often wondered how love clicked between Aditya and Priya. They were both so different in their opinions. Priya was so orthodox whereas Aditya was very modern in his views. Priya was so narrow-minded whereas Aditya was care free. Maybe unlike poles attract. Sid often mouthed it in front of Priya. He hated her as much as she hated him.

Talking about Aditya, he was brought up in Mumbai. His parents owned a very big and reputed textile business which would surely be under Aditya's control after his graduation. Like every rich businessman's kids, Aditya too had his schooling in an extraordinary boarding school. He had a lot of admirers in his school. He loved his school as much as he hated this college. Aditya's dad was always into business and he never had time for his family but whenever he was at home, they had so much fun together. He loved his family a lot though his father was a little strict.

Aditya didn't like his college days initially. Having studied in an extraordinary school near

Mumbai, he hated this college to the core. If at all there was a reason for him to go to college, it was Priya. Though Sid had been friends with him right from the start, he felt closer to Priya. Well... That was folly. He didn't know how much Sid knew and understood him. And it was Sid who had stood by Aditya whenever he was in trouble. Sid is a kind of person who would give anything for friendship.

As for Aditya, time seemed to fly when Priya was with him. She never bothered to tell about her to Aditya. She would say 'That's not important'. If he pestered her she would get irritated and fight with him.

For the past one month Priya's behavior towards Aditya had been really bizarre. She hated everything Aditya did that she had loved initially. She hated the limelight in which he sailed through smoothly. Though he was good she couldn't bring herself to love him. At last she realized the fact that it had just been a crush and that she had never loved him really.

As soon as college began that year they had begun fighting for all silly matters available on earth. She stopped attending his phone calls and didn't respond to him properly. She stared at him like a stranger in the corridors. Aditya was surprised by her strange behavior but he just thought she was really busy and stressed out due to over work.

Now, standing alone in the mall, he just wanted it all to be a dream and he said to himself that everything will be fine by tomorrow.

*****

'Aditya!' called a shrill voice.

Aditya looked up to see what had happened now. It was Ms. Kavita's class on Linear Integrated Circuits. The circuit diagrams on the black board showed that she had been teaching something on Phase Locked Loop. And the lecturer was of course glaring at him as if her gaze would turn him to ashes.

Ms. Kavita Ramanathan, ME was the most stern and morose looking staff in the otherwise easy going department of ECE.

She was of the opinion that the top scoring students were the brainy ones and the ones who had out of the box thoughts as being stupid. She hated Aditya because

i)   he was brilliant(this doesn't mean he is a top scorer),

ii) she couldn't find the answers for the questions he asked in her class,

iii) he missed most of her lectures this semester but still managed to understand all the concepts,

iv) he got the correct output for an experiment in the LIC lab for which she was sure no one would get the output.

And now he was caught not listening to her lecture. Well... This is not the first time he got caught.

'I called your name Aditya! And you are supposed to stand up. Do you expect me to teach this basic respect you are supposed to give your teachers? Is this what you learnt in school all these years?' asked Ms.Kavita. Aditya stood up and looked at her.

'Summarize what I've been teaching today' asked Ms.Kavita with an evil smile on her face. She looked like a cat which has just found its prey.

Sid was looking curiously at his friend because he has always come out with the correct answers for whatever this smug looking lecturer had fired at him.

'I'm sorry. I don't remember what…' said Aditya and the whole class gasped suddenly. Sid looked very surprised. He forgot to breathe for a few seconds. He started to whisper to Aditya about the circuits but Aditya stood still looking down at the desk.

'Look Mr.Aditya! If you are not interested in my class I give you full freedom to get out of my class. I don't want any mentally absent students in my class. Is this the way you respect your teachers?' shouted Ms.Kavita.

Aditya looked up and said 'Sorry!'

'You may be brilliant enough to be in the run for the secretary of the Robotics club. But that doesn't mean that you are brainy and that you should sit idle in the class room. I want you out of my class now' yelled Ms.Kavita.

'Sorry mam. I didn't mean to but I was disturbed…' said Aditya and Ms.Kavita's glare became sharper.

'My class hour is not when you can let your thoughts wander. I don't want to waste my time now on people like you. Meet me after the class in the staff room' said Ms.Kavita and added 'You may now sit down'.

Aditya sat down in his chair and Sid said 'It's okay buddy! That female is always like that'.

This incident resulted in the reduction of marks in the assignment submitted by Aditya. Well...The engineering college lecturers find only the internal assessment marks as their weapons against the students with whom they bore a grudge. And of course revenge is sweet.

Chapter 5

A week had passed. It was a Saturday evening. The weather was unusually parky. The grey clouds started gathering in the sky like tons of wool.

The college library was almost empty except for a few students who were browsing the internet. The cheerful looking librarian (Yes! Cheerful! This librarian is quite contrary.) was prowling among the books arranging them in order. Sarah stayed back longer that day to read some journals. She looked up and found that it was about to rain. The wind was strongly blowing. Her stomach grumbled in hunger as she had skipped her lunch to get a record note book signed. The lecturers in her department were particularly serious about getting the practical records signed in time.

Sarah stood up and prepared to leave.

'Leaving?' asked the librarian.

'Yeah! I think it's gonna rain. Bye!' replied Sarah.

She came out of the library, climbed down the spiral staircase and came out of the college. It began to drizzle and as usually she had no umbrella with her. Cold breeze hit her hard on her face and her face turned a light shade of pink. She was reminded of her hometown where it rains 24 x 7 and the weather is very pleasant. She smiled to herself as a thought crossed her mind 'I love this rain'. She had this strange thing for rain. Whenever she was happy she would love the rain and if she was in a bad mood she will curse the rain as if it was the rain that spoilt everything. She was shivering as she headed towards the canteen. There were beads of raindrops on her hair.

As soon as she reached the canteen she came face to face with the person whom she least wanted to meet on this planet ....Bharani and her gang...her least favourite seniors.

'Oh my God!' thought Sarah.

Sarah always had the bad luck of accidentally coming across people whom she did not want to meet at all and absolutely at the wrong time. It was Sarah's ill luck that Bharani also saw her entering the canteen and signaled to Sarah to come to her. Sarah approached them casually concealing her fear of what they would tell her that day. According to Sarah, Bharani looked like an overgrown cat.

'How many times have I told you not to wear this dress Sarah? It's too tight for you' said Bharani. Sarah really got annoyed.

'You have told that for every dress I wear. I don't understand why my dress bothers you' replied Sarah bringing together a little courage.

'How dare you speak like that to a senior? Is this how you respect your seniors?' asked the horse faced girl who was sitting to Bharani's right and was definitely one of her cronies.

'Respect? You should earn it. Don't beg for….'

At that exact moment a few boys from the basketball team entered the canteen after their practice session. It was beginning to rain heavily. Sid and Aditya were among the last few guys who came inside. They were all drenched in the rain. Aditya's hair looked cool with a wet look. He was spinning the ball on his finger balancing it on the top of his finger looking like a modern day's Greek God Atlas.

Sid saw Sarah and called out 'Hey kid! Come here'.

Sarah thanked every God for sending a savior and went to Sid without taking a second look at Bharani.

'Hi! And thank you for rescuing me, my knight in armour' said Sarah to Sid with relief. She smiled at them.

'Looks like you are knee deep in trouble already?' asked Sid jerking his head towards Bharani. He seemed happy to have rescued Sarah from Bharani.

'What shall I do? Trouble is chasing me like a mad dog wherever I go. My tagline is gonna be 'Wherever I go trouble follows!' Now, doesn't that suit me?' She pointed to Bharani and added 'First she told me not to smile. Second, she told me not to walk fast, then she told me not to reply back and if I kept quiet she demanded a reply and now she has got some problems with my dress' said Sarah with a big sigh.

'I told you not to smile too... at least at these girls. I know the girls here. They envy everything the other girls do...especially juniors. They just can't take in the fact that someone else is better than them in anything.' Sarah smiled again and said 'Sarah and her enigmatic smile'. Aditya who was keeping quiet all the time said 'Pull a chair and join us'.

Sarah dragged a nearby chair and joined them.

'Aditya, the song you sang for the cultural fest was awesome. Your song woke up Preethi from her deep sleep. And congrats guys for the first prize! I knew you would win.'

'Everyone liked the song except the one to whom it was intended to reach!' said Sid dryly.

'What?' exclaimed Sarah.

'Well. It was for his girlfriend and she hated the song' replied Sid.

'But why?' asked Sarah totally surprised.

'Because everyone liked it' winked Aditya.

'I am really sorry Aditya. But how could anyone hate that song!' said Sarah.

He smiled and said 'That's okay'.

Sarah added 'Did anyone tell you? Your voice is so like Enrique's. I dunno much about music but I love Enrique and Taylor Swift a lot.'

'You talk a lot too. I am sure I know why trouble chases you' said Sid and added 'You have that infectious happiness and charm about you.'

Sarah smiled not knowing how to respond.

Sid was rummaging through Aditya's bag.

'What are you searching for?' asked Aditya.

Sid took out a big block of chocolate from the bag and offered it to Sarah and said 'Let us be friends'.

Sarah happily accepted the chocolate and said 'It's strange. Why do you give chocolates for friendship? Anyway, thanks.'

'Haven't you seen the advertisements? It's called Shubh aarambh (good beginning)!' teased Sid.

Sarah started laughing, 'But I thought you would buy me lunch! That's okay' and added to Aditya 'Do you always carry chocolates?'

Thus began the entire story…with a sweet block of chocolate and a wholesome meal for Sarah.

*****

Chapter 6

'You're in the class
With a chalk piece
In your hand
You're trying to tell us
Something we wouldn't hear.
But you go on as if
We do hear.

We're in the class
It's a difficult situation
We are listening to your lecture
With no idea
What you were teaching
Just now.

But you are a genius;
We are foolish
You are a lecturer
And we are students.
Dreaming about the day
When we would finally wake up
To our senses.

*If you could make us grasp what you
teach everyday
And if you teach the way we want you
to teach
You'll be so sweet.*

*Taking the notes
With our heart and soul miles away
I can't help thinking but
This is how it shouldn't be
Dreaming all the time
And telling ourselves
Hey! Isn't this crazy?*

*And you've got a voice
That could make us all shut down
And we haven't listened to you
For weeks on end
But we do know that you are better than
that
Hey watcha doing to a class like us!*

*Teaching to our class
In the middle of the noon
You're the one who makes us sleep
When you know we're about to cry
We know your favourite words
And you tell us about our tests
Think I know where you belong
Think I know it's with the beasts*

*Don't you see that you're the one who
terrifies us
Been this way so long*

Now, why don't you see!
You are so mean.

You belong with the beasts!'

'What is this?' asked Aditya pointing to the paper which had the above song.

'A remake version of Taylor Swift's You belong with me! How's it?' asked Sarah proudly and Preethi backed her saying 'That's really cool.'

Sid took the paper and made funny faces while reading it.

Aditya said 'Insane!'

It did not take long for Sid, Aditya, Sarah and Preethi to hang out together. It looked like they had been friends all their lives. They found themselves very happy in each other's company. They met in the canteen almost every evening and shared their top stories of the day. Sid bought a chocolate for Sarah every day before he learnt that she hated chocolates. Sid became Sarah's 'Bhaiya' (big brother) soon. Sarah pestered him calling 'Bhaiya... Bhaiya'. And Sid quite liked it having no siblings himself. He called Sarah a 'kid' and Preethi as 'goofy'.

Sid and Preethi fought every day. Sarah narrated funny stories for which only she laughed. The look on Preethi's face on hearing Sarah's so called jokes would make the others laugh. Sid usually liked to hear the girls' hostel adventures. He particularly liked the one in which Sarah locked the warden inside her room and the other where Preethi directed a frog straight to the warden's room.

Sarah talked nonstop which made Aditya call her a 'prototype of some unearthly species'. He began to like her very much. Sarah noticed that though he laughed along with them he was sad whenever he came across Priya. His laugh was hollow without any life. Aditya felt much lighter when they were around but he had an empty feeling as if he had lost something that belonged to him a long time ago and he was very angry with himself that he began to blame himself for everything that went wrong. Once Sarah got told off by a professor for she had been five minutes late for the lecture. She had gone to lunch with the others and lost track of time. She was upset a bit about that since she was marked absent for the whole afternoon session. Aditya felt himself responsible for that and refused to talk to her for one full day. Though everyone was with him he began to feel left out. He had a feeling that he was lonely… sailing across an endless ocean alone. Sarah along with Sid tried their level best to cheer him up. Sarah hadn't seen his impressive smile for ages and she yearned for it. The more the efforts the three put to make Aditya happy the more it went in vain as he tried to be very much unhappy as possible and he hurt anyone if they tried.

If they were free in the weekends, they went out together in Sid's car. Yes. Sid owned a car. It was a birthday present from his dad on his twentieth birthday. Aditya had a car too…Skoda and he never revealed his possession to his friends because his mother had denied him to drive the car on an everyday basis. So he either came to college in the college bus or with Sid. Mostly with Sid. Nowadays people were least bothered about Sarah and her smile or even her dresses since she was friends with Sid and Aditya. Even Priya began to smile at Sarah even though she completely ignored Aditya.

But Aditya was not the same anymore after Priya's engagement. When he saw the glint of gold on her finger two days after her engagement when they were all having lunch in the café, he walked out of the café angrily and did not return back to college that day. The three of them looked at each other helplessly.

All the three of them did whatever Aditya liked to make him happy when they discovered that he was depressed. Sarah felt bad that he was very unhappy. She didn't want to lose any of her friends at any cost. She didn't know his love story and had no interest in it either. Sid had told her some parts of it and she didn't wish to hear more. From the day she had met Aditya, she had a special liking for him. It increased day by day as Sid told her whatever Aditya had done for Priya. But she was angry with Priya too as she had made him what he was not. Though Sarah admired Aditya's love she hated it because of one fact... he had hurt himself a lot in many instances. Sid didn't like Priya and so he didn't comment on this break up. Few days went by, Aditya preferred to be alone these days and Sarah would look at him with an innocent face as he left as if it would persuade him to stay back.

Aditya commented 'That puppy dog look is not gonna persuade me to stay back.'

Sid noticed this change in Sarah and one day said to Aditya, 'I think Sarah loves you'.

'What are you talking about?' laughed Aditya.

'It's true man!'

'She is a kid. Maybe she is just confused.'

'Well buddy! She is not a kid. Maybe she is innocent but definitely not childish. She is far better in many ways. You should open your eyes and look who really cares for you.'

'You know very well how much I did for Priya. I spent a lot, bunked classes and lied to mum and dad and you know how many times I have escorted her to her home town. Why did I do all these? I didn't want to lose her but now… I was true to her all the time!' shouted Aditya holding his head in his hands looking totally mad. He stopped middle way as he saw Sarah coming.

'Cool down! I have told you earlier. You deserve someone much better' said Sid.

'It's high time you moved on Aditya' said Sarah slowly and placed her hand carefully on his and gave it a squeeze. But she was scared that he might get angry for having touched him but he merely smiled at her sorrowfully.

'Shall we go for a movie this weekend?' asked Sid to Sarah to change the topic of their conversation so that the tension will subside.

'Sorry... I am not coming. Internal assessment exams are nearing' said Sarah and added 'I am going to Preethi's home today. Can anyone drop me in the nearest bus stop? I just missed the college bus while searching for you guys. Here is your book Sid Bhaiya!' said Sarah handing over a book to Sid.

'Aditya will do the honor. His home is very near to Preethi's. And stop calling me Bhaiya. It makes me feel old' said Sid playfully while he enjoyed it.

'Bhaiya... Bhaiya... Bhaiya...' went on Sarah trying to irritate Sid.

Sarah looked at Aditya doubtfully whether he would refuse. But to her surprise he called 'Come on Sarah! Let's go'.

Sarah couldn't feel free to talk to Aditya as she could with Sid. She was scared that he would find out somehow that she liked him. She knew very well that she looked upon Sid as a brother and a best friend and she also knew it was not the same with Aditya. After hearing what Sid said about Sarah being in love, Aditya was confused too. He liked her a lot and knew she cared for him a lot but how could this be love? Today he felt like he wanted to talk his heart out to this little girl who was in love with him. It was his duty to make her realize that she was making the worst mistake in her life.

'Sarah! I need to talk to you. Can we go somewhere?'

'Sure!'

He drove to a nearby park. Sarah was standing next to his bike and Aditya was leaning on a nearby tree. She waited for him to begin the conversation but he did not. So she did.

'Shall we walk?'

He didn't reply but they started walking.

'Do you live with your parents?' asked Sarah.

'No. They are in Mumbai. But my mom visits me often. My parents are into textile business. Very rich people. I am their only son and as you can see, a spoilt brat', replied Aditya with a sarcastic smile.

'You are not spoilt!'

Aditya returned a weak smile.

'Am I your friend?' asked Sarah.

'What a question to ask? Of course little devil! You are my friend as much as Sid is'.

'Can you tell me about you and Priya?'

Silence.

A long silence.

During that moment Sarah felt she had better not asked.

Aditya took a deep breath and said 'I don't know why I am telling you this but I feel it's my duty to warn you. When I was in the first year I didn't like the college. No friends. I was brought up in Mumbai and everything was different here. It was my decision to come here for college but I hated this place right from the day I came. Even you would have experienced the same, right?'

Sarah nodded a 'yes'.

Aditya's story goes like…

'I missed my school days in Mumbai a lot. How different life was! I began to miss my school friends a lot. Life was going on so dry and all. One day when

I was returning from the library I heard a sweet voice calling out 'Aditya!'

I turned to see who it was. A girl, in a bright green salwar and most probably of my age was walking towards me. She had long hair which was neatly plaited. I have never in my life liked girls with long hair and the ones that wear all these fluorescent colored salwars. But there was something different about her. The first thing that came to my mind was 'She is beautiful'. I had dropped my id card and she had called me to hand it to me.

We got introduced to each other and we came to know that we had chatted in Orkut, the social networking site where almost everyone in the college had a login account. We spoke for a while about the college and then I realized I was going to be late for the class if I stayed there anymore. So I said 'Bye Priya! Hope we'll meet again soon'. She smiled and went away. I ran back to my class and was just in time for Professor Rajan's lecture on Fundamentals of Computing.

Professor Rajan is a mad man. He keeps threatening students with words like detention, suspension, expulsion. I guess he has some affinity for the suffix –sion. He was half bald and if he ever walked in open sunlight people would wonder whether he had tied a mirror to his head. He was as thin as a coat hanger and his clothes hung loosely about him. His trademark shirt colors were pale blue and postcard yellow with a black or brown pant and a tie which never suited him. Sid had named him as 'postcard'. He always had red kumkum on his forehead (students commented it as the traffic signal). He had done Masters in Computer Science & engineering and he was of the opinion that he was the best teacher available in the entire college.

But please don't think he teaches well! Because he doesn't. Well… Considering some other lecturer's way of teaching he's comparatively better. That's it. That's the only compliment we can give him. He turns to the board and for almost half an hour writes some notes and orders the students to take it down. When the time of his hour is about to get over he turns to the students and reads out whatever he wrote on the board. He reads them thrice as if we couldn't read it on our own and he finishes his so called lecture taking half of the lunch hour away and getting as many curses from the hungry students as possible. According to him his students

a) Should never be late even if he is in a meeting with the principal.
b) Should never score below 85 in the assessments.
c) Should never take leave without his consent.
d) Should write down every word he utters in the class.

He likes to punish students and enjoy watching them getting into trouble. And he is a kind of professor who makes mountains out of mole hills like-

'You are suspended for a week for talking in my classes',

'Go! Bring your parents. Only then I will permit you inside my class',

'You just earned a week's detention for not wishing me in the corridor'.

One word to describe him… 'Sadist'.

I was just in time for the class and Sid was sitting beside me. And as usual the professor was writing on the board. And everyone was busy taking notes.

'I met this girl Priya near the library. I don't know why but I couldn't stop thinking about her. I like her a lot', I said to Sid.

'You just met her, didn't you?' asked Sid.

'But we have chatted in Orkut earlier' I replied.

Professor Rajan turned to the students with a smile on his face and said in a sing song tone 'How many times should I warn you students? I don't want anyone talking when I am writing on the board. Don't think I am funny. I just keep smiling when I scold. Don't take advantage of it.' He turned to the board again to continue his writing.

'Are you mad? You like that female whom you met just seconds ago?' asked Sid.

'Yes. And you can call me whatever you want to but that is not gonna change my mind' replied Aditya.

'Go to hell. I don't care what crap you do but seriously Priya is a really bad choice for you. Are you seriously gonna date her?' asked Sid.

'Don't talk as if you know her.'

'I've known her my entire life. She was in my school. The only girl I loathed in my life and still do. She has the thought that she is the only correct person living on earth. And she hates me to the core since I was the only one who retorted to everything she said and made her see sense.'

'I don't care. I like her and I am gonna tell her that' I hissed.

Professor Rajan finished writing on the board and was preparing to read what he had written on the board.

Sid whispered to me 'You choose your fate!'

And I met her in the canteen a few days later and we exchanged our mobile numbers. And you can understand where this is heading to, Sarah. It became like a second's separation from her made me go mad. She was so sweet. I don't remember when it happened but it just happened as in fairy tales when Prince Charming meets the Princess. Anyway I hate fairy tales. I proposed to her one day. She just smiled. She told me she didn't have to say that and that love is supposed to be felt. We hung around together in our second year. She told me once that I made her feel really special when I bunked my class to give her a send off to her home town. I still feel like it all happened yesterday.'

'I never kept a record of how much I spent on her phone bills, chocolates, gifts. And money doesn't matter but the fact that I lied to my mom to get the money hurts me badly these days. I have not been true to my mom who loves me a lot. I bunked my classes and risked everything in my college life just to drop her in the bus terminus. I could have been expelled for all these. How can she forget all this Sarah?'

'We started fighting after a girl in her class told her that she has a crush on me. Well… That's not my fault. Priya could have told her that she loves me but she didn't want to spoil her reputation. And then the basketball tournament followed. She didn't want me to go but I am a player since school days and I can't sit tight without playing and all. She almost stopped talking to me after that. And then you… you know what happened in the mall. She is telling me now that I am messing up with her life and that I should leave. Funny, isn't it?'

Sarah was a very good listener. She was patiently listening as Aditya poured his heart out to her.

'And after the fourth semester exams, we went for a movie…her selection. The theatre was half empty…you would never have seen such a boring movie in your life. But she loved it. She kissed me that day.' A smile spread on his face. Sarah noticed how he enjoyed narrating everything in detail about Priya.

'He must have loved her so much. How silly falling in love with a person who doesn't love you back' thought Sarah.

Sarah could see how happy he was when he spoke about Priya and she pitied him. She didn't feel anything special about Priya. How could he have fallen for such a plain girl? Is this why people say

'Love is blind'? But can love be this very blind… how could Aditya for this matter have been so mad about a girl who was so like just another girl?

Sarah smiled too. But she felt a pang of jealousy over Priya. She envied Priya. 'How could she have hurt Aditya? I don't know what's happening to me but the more I come to know of his love for Priya the more I start loving him. This is madness. I shouldn't get caught in this mess' thought Sarah.

Aditya continued, 'That was the first and the last time she didn't fight with me. That day when she bid goodbye to me she was almost in tears. One month… I couldn't imagine how I survived without seeing her. I was so obsessed with her. I shouldn't have been so dependent on her. I realize my fault now but it's too late. I don't know what happened to her during the holidays. After that she became possessive and started to misunderstand me totally. She found fault with me for everything and when I tried to make her realize I loved only her she began to ignore me as if I was inexistent. And finally the day we met in the mall that was the last of this epic love story. She announced her marriage with a London groom.'

'She's getting married! You never told any of us!' exclaimed Sarah stressing on every syllable she uttered. Aditya hadn't told anyone that was the reason why he's upset.

'Yes, she's getting married!'

'But why, Aditya?'

Silence again ruled.

'I guess… she never loved me.'

'What makes you say that?' wondered Sarah.

'I understood it recently. She insisted on being friends and it was I who persuaded her to move our relationship a bit further. And I am really sorry about it now. I should have waited.'

'What difference would it have made?'

'Please Sarah. I don't want to proceed with the details any further. Let's drop this topic. I don't want to think about it again.'

Sarah's eyes filled with tears.

She said 'Sorry Aditya!'

But her mind was racing fast. She thought the way a small kid would have thought about bringing two friends together after a fight for a candy, 'There's still time. I can talk to Priya about this and convince her to come back. That will definitely bring Aditya back to normal.'

'What are you thinking?' asked Aditya reading her mind and added 'And you little devil! Please don't try to do what you are thinking.'

'You know what Aditya... Priya is very unlucky to have lost a guy like you. Seriously... if it had been me I would never have left you. Any girl would love you Aditya. You know what? My co-bencher Maya has a crush on you too!' said Sarah trying to cheer him up.

'Co bencher?' asked Aditya.

'The one who sits beside me in class' replied Sarah.

Aditya smiled at Sarah and said 'Ha! That's sweet. Anyway thanks for the compliment. But... I will tell you one more thing Sarah. Don't waste your time on me. I am a total loser. It's better if you keep away from me. Don't get into trouble because of me. And don't get hurt. This was all my fault and I can perfectly handle it. So please don't confuse yourself. Understood?' asked Aditya.

Sarah nodded a 'yes' and after a moment's silence Aditya said 'Come! I'll drop you home.'

They didn't talk to each other until they reached Preethi's home.

'I haven't told this to anyone…not even Sid knows what actually happened. He loathes her a lot. My mom knows Priya but they haven't yet met. My mom wanted to meet her this time when she comes but…' said Aditya.

'Just give me a call if you feel lonely. Remember you always can count me your friend. And we are all there for you' said Sarah and gave a pat on his arm.

He smiled and rode away in his bike.

Sarah stood there watching him ride away. She felt different today. She felt closer than anyone else to Aditya today. Actually she felt special for Aditya had confided in her. 'Even if he doesn't love me, he does consider me his friend. That is enough for me' thought Sarah.

She was sure that she was falling head over heels in love with someone she should not be falling in love… with Aditya. Maybe, tomorrow will never be the same.

*****

Chapter 7

By nine, the next morning, Preethi's family had gone for work into the hustle and bustle of the city and the two- Preethi and Sarah were left alone at home as usual. Preethi was lying on the bed with a book which was about the weight of a brick and she was trying to read it and taking a sip from the bottle of Coca-Cola. 'Coca-Cola' almost was the staple food of Preethi. She lived by drinking only that and Sarah often voiced how Preethi alone could survive like that. The music was on in a high pitch. It was some Avril Lavigne song- Preethi's favourite. Sarah was sitting in a high backed chair half sleeping.

Sarah called lazily 'Preethi!'

'What?'

'Yesterday Aditya told me his love story.'

'Sarah! Are you drunk?' asked Preethi.

'NO! Why?' screamed Sarah alarmed at Preethi's question.

'Because if you count this once you have told me this statement at least a thousand hundred and eighty seven times. But you deny me the details.'

'Oh! It's nothing. I'll tell you later', said Sarah and let out a sigh.

'Croak croak' went Sarah's mobile phone. Its name was 'croaky'. Of course it was Sarah who did the honor of christening it with that name.

'Where is my croaky?' searched Sarah. It was lying under the pillow on which Preethi was resting.

Preethi handed over croaky to Sarah saying 'Call from Sid!'

Sarah picked it up and said 'Bhaiya!'

'Hey kid! I'm in Aditya's place. Can you come along here for a moment please?'

'Why? What's the matter?'

'Well… He is just upset.'

'Anything serious?'

'No. Actually I want to set certain things straight. I need to talk to you.'

'Yeah! I'm coming.'

She checked herself in the mirror once and gave some final touches to her hair that fell just below her shoulders. Unusually she had done her eye lining job better that day.

'Preethi! I am going to Aditya's house. Tell me the way.'

'It's just a two minute walk from here. Go straight down the street and take the third left. The seventh house on the right is his. Any problem?'

'I smell something fishy.'

'You want me to come?'

'Nopes. I'll manage. You continue sleeping.'

*****

Aditya's house was pretty big. Sid's car was parked outside the gate. As she opened the gate she could hear a loud bark from somewhere in the house.

'That must be Orion!' thought Sarah. Aditya had told her about his pet dog Orion.

She had a pet at her home too. A Labrador. Its name was 'Sirius'. Well… Sarah was a Harry Potter fan. Also she loved star gazing in summer.

The front of the house had a beautiful garden with roses and crotons. The lawn was neatly mown and maintained. Sarah wondered how rich he should be to maintain the house where he lived alone. But she hated rich people. Sarah rang the door bell and Sid opened it.

'Come in. Didn't Preethi come with you?' asked Sid grimly and let her in.

'She was sleeping. So I left her at home. Well… What is it that you wanted to talk that couldn't wait till Monday?'

'You will see. You spoke to him regarding Priya yesterday?' asked Sid and led her to Aditya's room. The hall was really big and it had a large vessel with water in which flowers were floating in the middle of the room. Sid led her upstairs to Aditya's room.

'Yes. Because I thought it would be a relief if he just confided in someone…' and her voice stuck middle way as she saw a scene that she would never forget in her lifetime. The room which she was about to enter was very different. Though the situation in which she found herself standing was terrible she couldn't help wondering about the room she was about to enter. She couldn't find words to describe it. On a corner was a table with books the size of a pillow stacked on it. Aditya's black bag embossed with the Batman symbol was lying on the chair nearby. The lab coat was on the hanger. Other than this the room had a full stock of curious stuff which reflected Robotics… Aditya's passion. It was an otherwise beautiful room but now it really looked gloomy. It was not the room that had made her speechless. In the middle of this museum, Aditya was sitting on his bed. His wrist was bandaged. And the smell in the room made Sarah nauseous… tobacco! Sarah was not that very dull headed not to realize what had happened. His eyes were bloodshot. He had not slept all night. Had he been through drugs? She hoped against hopes that he hadn't. There were marks on his face where tears had dried. As a whole he looked like a psycho. As he saw Sarah coming he shouted at Sid 'Why did you bring her into trouble now? You better leave Sarah! Please leave me alone.'

Sid ignored his shout totally.

Sarah couldn't move a muscle. She stood in the doorway looking unbelievably at Aditya. Rich people have too many problems in life.

'We just came from the hospital' said Sid and took Sarah inside the room and locked the door behind and added 'The servant is on leave today.'

'What happened? Don't tell me you're through drugs' said Sarah to Aditya after a long time.

'No! Thank God he didn't. He didn't want to kill himself either. Look! That's why he had carefully crafted the cut in his wrist. The doc is a family friend. He saved us from all the trouble. But anyway my mom will come to know of this' said Sid in a tone that expressed total contempt. Sarah only knew too well that Sid was mad because he had a great contempt for Priya and it hurt him a lot to see his best friend Aditya like this.

'Why did you do this Aditya? You were alright yesterday. What happened then?' asked Sarah, her voice almost a whisper now for she was very heartbroken.

'You can't understand Sarah. You don't have any idea how much it hurts when someone you trusted totally just threw you away like you are vermin.'

'Don't try to teach me lessons Aditya. You didn't know her long, did you? Stop taking all the blame upon you and for heaven's sake stop fooling yourself. Do you think we are all enjoying ourselves when you are like this? Everyone has his own problems in life. I was supposed to become a surgeon just like my mom. But look at me. Well... I am not and I hate myself for that. Did I go kill myself for that?'

'We are all so depressed. Do you know why? Because you are unhappy. Well... You wouldn't have had time to analyze all this. I have been yearning to see you laugh for ages. We all have been. Where has that awesome smile of yours gone? Now don't ask us to leave you alone. We won't. We have realized now that we have done a great mistake by letting you alone on your own when you had actually needed us. Ask Sid. We are all your friends Aditya. We will be with you all the time. You can't ditch us just like that.'

'Sarah! It hurts a lot. I couldn't sleep. Yes, it's true I don't want to die. But everything around me is killing me. Every moment I'm dying. My mind wouldn't just rest. I want some peace of mind. For the past one week I have been taking sleeping pills to fall asleep. Don't you people see? I am very depressed. You guys can't help me out. I am beyond every levels of disappointment' said Aditya and pointing to his hand he added 'This physical pain can keep my mind off her for a while. At least this is bearable.'

'You have no rights to tell us what we are capable of. So you have such a poor opinion about your friends Aditya! I can't believe this. This can't be you Aditya! Don't talk like a philosopher. We want our Aditya back! You can't just take him away from us, hurt him and kill him in the process gradually. Don't you realize, idiot? We need you Aditya.'

Silence prevailed for a few seconds.

Few drops of tear fell to the floor from Sarah's eyes.

'I just wanted to see her one last time. But she didn't want to see me again. So I thought this at least would bring her to me but I now realize that nothing will bring her back. I have lost her forever' said Aditya.

'One last time? Why would you say that? You wanted to end your life? Your life has not ended with Priya. She is not your life's statement. You are just twenty one. You are smart, handsome, brainy and all that. Why don't you show her your attitude if she does it to you?'

Sarah went on since Aditya did not say anything. 'She doesn't deserve you Aditya! Why don't you understand? She is not worth your love. I really admire your love. Anyone will, if they knew you. You just loved the wrong person. If she is being practical with her decisions and wants to look past your love I want you to prove that you can very well get along without her. Why do you hurt yourself for what is not your fault?'

'If you really loved someone let them choose their ways. If your love comes back to you it is always yours. If not then it was never yours. Divert your mind into something useful. Live your life. Don't hurt us all.'

Sarah walked towards Aditya and knelt down beside him. She grabbed his collar and cried 'Do you want to rob the happiness out of us all Aditya? Is this the end...the end of everything? Don't you realize? We'll be there for you when you are in need.'

Tears dropped from her eyes and rolled down her cheeks. He looked into her eyes and realized his foolishness. Tears filled his eyes and he was ashamed of himself. He pulled her into a tight hug as she cried. He patted her head as she cried and tried to console her.

'Sarah! I am… I'm really sorry. I will never hurt you again. I mean it. Please don't cry. I trust you. Everything will be fine'. He added to Sid 'Tell her Sid! I won't do this again. I just need some time but I'll definitely go on well. I'll try my best guys. Trust me!'

Sid was wondering how the kid in Sarah had suddenly vanished. He smiled at Aditya, nodded and said 'Yes, buddy!' This trust was the beginning of everything.

*****

Chapter 8

After a week…
On Monday, the internal assessment exams began. Everyone in college seemed to be so active all of a sudden. The hidden cameras in every classroom were activated to catch the ones who cheat in the exams red handedly. One could find a student or two making suggestions about what questions have the highest probability for being asked in the exam. A few students were cursing the education system for making them learn essays of ten pages length by heart as they were reading. Sarah was sitting in a silent corner of her classroom with her classmates and Preethi was with her classmates. 'I could rather have read this topic than having slept for two hours in the afternoon' cursed Preethi under her breath.

By a quarter to nine, everyone assembled in their respective exam halls. Preethi was supposed to go to the first floor and Sarah to the second floor. To her surprise, she found that she was seated adjacent to Aditya.

Aditya smiled at Sarah. She asked 'Studied?'

He nodded 'No, But I can get through.'

She smiled and gave his hand a squeeze.

He looked better than the other day she had seen him at his home. He had actually started to try and take Priya out of his minds.

Though Sid and he had often commented on Sarah's smile as being so girly, for the first time he noticed how beautiful Sarah looked when she smiled. She was not a kid after all like they commented her.

Sarah's soft hair hung over her face and touched her shoulders gently. She was dressed up in a white salwar and looked really pretty like a little angel that had fallen to the earth. Whenever she bent down to write, her hair kept falling over her face which she slowly slid behind her ear on the left.

For a moment he forgot where he was. Everyone except him was busy writing. When he realized what he had been doing he smiled to himself and thought, 'Now I understand what life is all about. She made me realize it.'

For every once in a few minutes he would look up and see Sarah. He realized that it made him feel better.

After the exam, he rushed out to find Sid. He found him in the landing of the first floor.

'Hey dude!' he called.

Sid showed thumbs down and said 'No hope! You?'

'I will fail decently'. Both of them walked towards the parking lot.

'Hey buddy! I wanted to tell you something...' said Aditya.

'Again? Shoot it!'

'I love Sarah.'

'So does everyone.'

'I meant... I love her. I want to marry her and share the rest of my life with her. I want her to be happy throughout her life.'

'Did you hit your head accidentally or is it the exam that's doing this to you?' asked Sid flabbergasted.

'Stop kidding Sid. I am serious.'

'Man! You are mad. Totally mad. Only a week back you almost killed yourself for some Priya and now you tell me that you love Sarah. I am sure it's the aftermath of the question paper. You will be fine soon, mate.'

'Sid! I loved Priya. I realized my madness when Sarah cried for me that day. Priya is a shadow of the past...a passing cloud maybe. It still does hurt when I think about her. But now when I think about how I had been madly in love with someone who had stopped loving me ages ago for some reason I don't even know I feel so stupid. Though it will take time for me to recover fully I am saying you the truth buddy, I do care for Sarah a lot. When she hugged me that day I saw her love for me shine in her eyes. She has been trying to hide it from me for ages but she is really a very bad actress.'

Aditya added 'That moment, I decided that even if she rejects me I won't feel bad because I know that she cares too. That's enough for me. She told me that she will be there for me and I know she really meant it. That day I wanted to meet Priya so badly that I cut my wrist and called her up. I just wanted to meet her once but she didn't bother. Instead it was Sarah and you who came rushing for help. That was the day I realized that people will be there around us when we are happy but only one out of the crowd will be equally ready to wipe your tears and stand up for you when you are not your own self. And Sid, I found my true love a week ago.'

'Aditya! You want Sarah to be happy? Then please don't make her choose you. You know very well you're a jerk' commented Sid and murmured to himself 'I hate the idea of both of you romancing around gluey eyed and all. Even the thought of it makes me sick.'

'Oh come on Sid! We won't behave like those fools you describe. Try to understand.'

'I was just kidding dude!' replied Sid and gave his friend a friendly shove.

*****

Chapter 9

For Sarah, nothing was remarkable except the weather....

It had changed from rainy to chilly. As December approached, along came the semester exams. So everyone was busy with his own work.

Sarah, Preethi, Sid and Aditya planned to go out on Christmas Eve as the exams got over on the twenty third. Aditya called up Sarah to wish her luck for her exams. And she kept asking 'How are you Addie?' whenever he called. He hated it when people called him 'Addie'. But since it was Sarah who called it was ok for him.

His usual answer was... 'Much better than yesterday.'

As Christmas neared, the merriment showed up in the air. Though the exams were going on, there was a holiday spree among the students.

But the city didn't show much of the Christmas spirit. Well... This is Chennai. Not New York. Only the big shopping malls and the air conditioned shops with giant glass doors were sporting a Christmas look.

On Christmas, the Santhome cathedral is the place one should not miss in a hurry. The beautiful cathedral looked elegant and regal and the choir was at its best. The sunlight brightens the inside of the cathedral as it enters through the multicolored glass windows. The cathedral itself is a masterpiece. The crucifixion of the Christ is depicted by wooden carvings hung on the walls of the cathedral. The giant crib with baby Jesus kept in the church is really a beauty to watch.

At the city center complex, in the basement, a huge Christmas tree decorated with lights and silvery stars was placed. Nearby was a Santa Claus statue made of plaster of paris. Father Christmas looked as merry as he can be. And there was also a snow man. The mall was crowded and there was a game show going on conducted by some leading television music channel.

And then there is the Marina beach which will be haunted on weekends as well as all the holidays. For the tourists, Chennai means Marina beach and a few landmarks. But most of the residents of Chennai preferred staying away from this particular beach except for the early birds (which includes mostly the old people who go for a walk or taking a laughter therapy) because all the other time the beach will be exclusively haunted by lovers. You can find them just everywhere… behind the boat, under the scorching sun, playing in water; building sand castles... just everywhere you turn your head.

The coffee shop perched in a comfortable corner of the city was a place where the ambience was always soothing and romantic. Being the Christmas Eve the shop was decorated in such a way that even a normal passerby would want to stop and behold the ornate shop for a while.

The Christmas tree in the shop was adorned with very small gift boxes wrapped in red and silver and little golden stars that sparkled in the dimly lit room. Two small kids about two years old were standing near the tree trying to pull away the gift boxes. They were twins and their mom was evidently tired of trying to beckon them back to their chairs.

The bell fixed over the door of the shop gave a tiny ring as someone entered. Well... it was Sarah, Preethi, Aditya and Sid. Even as they entered Sarah and Aditya were having a heated argument about something.

'I said I want an ice cream. But this is a coffee shop' sighed Sarah.

'Trust me! This place is good' replied Aditya.

'I wanted an icecream and not a frappe!' retorted Sarah. Aditya didn't reply but he was a bit worried as Sarah was discontent about not going to the ice cream shop on their way. They took their seats near the largest glass window in view of the small garden outside the shop. One of the twins ran towards Sarah and tugged her dress smiling at her. Sarah held the kid's hand and smiled back at it. Preethi showed funny faces and the kid began to laugh. The kid's mom came and lifted the hyperactive tiny tot in her arms, smiled at Sarah and went back to her table near the Christmas tree where the other twin was now examining the table cloth.

This distraction had taken Sarah's mind off her argument and she was smiling. Aditya was happy that she had forgotten the ice cream. Sometimes she could be very adamant. Very adamant, of course. A few days back when they had gone to attend a tech fest in a nearby college in the city, Aditya had walked to the next bus stop which took him nearly five minutes to reach by walk to get her an icecream otherwise she refused to talk to anyone. But when he began his walk, she protested but her eyes shone with happiness when he was back. The happiness was not because of the icecream but because he had actually bothered to walk so long to get it for her. That made her feel quite special. He was ready to do anything to make her smile… to make her happy after all that she had done to make him live. It wasn't that very hard doing it. She loved every small thing he did for her. He called her a 'Cruel girl'.

Sid commented 'That kid found the kindergarten girl in our gang to play with…. Birds of same feather.'

Preethi was laughing funnily.

Sid added, 'And kids really do love monkeys like Preethi. That kid really seemed to be wondering how you are not in the zoo.'

Preethi scowled at him.

Both of them started arguing about who was the real monkey. Their fight continued even after they had placed their orders and after the cappuccino and espressos came. Words like 'ape, chimpanzee etc' was in the air as they fought silently.

Aditya was silent throughout their fight as he was busy admiring Sarah. Sarah could feel his gaze on her that made her cheeks almost to burn red and she deliberately avoided his eyes and kept herself busy with the coffee and the music that was played in the shop and tried to look out at the garden. It wasn't that very easy to avoid his eyes but it was very difficult to meet them too. Her heart beat would redouble if she did that. It did whenever she saw him these days.

'I don't know how you guys prefer espressos over cappuccino' commented Preethi with a disgusted look at Sid and Aditya's cup of espresso.

'Cappuccino is for girls' retorted Sid.

Sid and Preethi's fight had ended finally and the conversation drifted to festivals and celebrations.

'Valentine's day is my favourite. I enjoy watching pretty girls looking at me expectantly...' said Sid with dreamy eyes.

'Don't expect too much Sid. Girls do think about Raksha Bandhan on seeing you. Have you ever proposed a girl in your lifetime?' teased Preethi.

'No. Haven't met one that very impressive' replied Sid with a sigh.

'Well... I warn you not to try. I can't imagine you doing that. You'll look so funny!' said Preethi with a laugh imagining how Sid would look if he held a rose and proposed a girl. She couldn't control her laughter.

'Since you warn me, I am gonna try. And you are gonna be my specimen Preethi. And beware of me. You might fall for me' said Sid. For this Sarah and Preethi burst into laughter.

Sid took the spoon from Sarah's cup and held it like a rose almost hitting Preethi with the spoon in the process and looked at her and said 'I love you' in a whisper as if he was in his death bed. Sid looked so sheepish. The girls burst into splits of laughter. 'Please Sid! Don't ever try that again in your life' laughed Sarah. 'You should understand Sarah! It was Preethi. And I didn't want her to be impressed by me you see. If I had shown her my real talent in proposing she might fall head over heels in love with me. That would really be a tragedy as you very well know. Once there was a girl who followed me wherever I went carrying a placard saying 'Marry me Sid! Please!' Crazy fans!' replied Sid. Aditya was busy admiring Sarah's ringing laughter. She hadn't laughed for ages and he felt guilty that he had been the reason for that.

And suddenly…

'Sarah!' called Aditya gently. His voice rang in her ears. Sarah looked up. Even Sid and Preethi stopped fighting and looked at him as if he had suddenly materialized among them. Aditya took Sarah's hand and held it between his palms, looked into her eyes and said 'When we first met, I never thought I'd be saying this to you. You are funny, charming and everything that I love.

I love you for who you are and what you made me. I love you and I can't stay away from you anymore!'

Sarah was looking unbelievably at Aditya.

Aditya just went on, 'I love the way you look at me. I love your smile. I love your silly talks. I just love everything you do. I love you Sarah!'

He sounded earnest.

Silence.

Except for the 'Liar!' from Preethi 'You love your guitar'. Sid suppressed her voice with his 'Shh'.

'Say something!' said Aditya.

Sarah was obviously very surprised that she couldn't find her voice. But her eyes said it all. It was full of tears and she had gone very pink.

'Stop staring like you don't know what I'm talking about. I can see the smile hidden behind those little lips. C'mon let it out!' smiled Aditya as Sarah was looking at him as if she hadn't heard him properly.

She finally smiled and managed to say, 'Aditya… I don't know what I should say to this … but you know the truth. I'm scared of being in love. After all the pains it caused you, it was not a good example, was it?'

'Well… As you say I know the truth of course. You love me too. Why don't you just say it now?' smiled Aditya looking at her expectantly.

Sarah took a deep breath.

After a moment's silence…

She looked into Aditya's eyes and said 'I don't want to love you but I do too!'

As she said this he could feel her cold palm within his palms. He kissed the tips of her fingers and she blushed once again. She went so pink that she looked like some kind of doll.

When they were leaving the coffee shop Sid asked Preethi, 'Why didn't you propose love to me?'

'Because I don't love you.'

'Thanks. I don't love you either' replied Sid and added to Aditya putting a hand over his shoulder 'So buddy… You finally got the courage'.

'No. I couldn't hide it anymore' replied Aditya.

*****

Nobody was in sight in the place where Aditya and Sarah went for a long walk hand in hand that day. Sid had taken Preethi for a movie of his type… fight, action, bloodshed and chases. He had decided to escape from Aditya and Sarah's romance episode. And he wanted to take revenge on Preethi for once she had made him spend two hundred bucks on a romantic movie. He hated such movies and called them soapy. According to him a movie's essential aspects were guns, machines, bloodshed, muscular men swearing heartily etc. You won't like to hear more about his type of movies. I'm sure you got the picture of those movies.

Sarah was unusually quiet that day. She hadn't got over the shock of Aditya's proposal. She had been in love with him for ages… From the day she had seen him sing, her heart had started to beat like drums whenever she saw him. She would be so scared whether people around her would realize it too. But she never imagined that he would fall in love with her. And now as they walked across the silent street together, Aditya took her hand in his and held it tightly. She looked up at him. He smiled his most charming smile for which she had fallen head over heels in love with him. The charming smile that had eluded her for a long time.

Cool breeze from the sea was blowing. The sky unusually gathered grey clouds. And then, all of a sudden pitter patter came the rain. The deserted street looked like some eighteenth century landscape. Sarah remembered the cover picture of a book she had read some time before.

The empty street had a closed shop in front of which Aditya and Sarah took shelter from the rain. In front of the shop was a huge tree that shielded the shop from the rain. Sarah stood leaning on the wall of the shop. The rain drops that had fallen on Aditya's hair sparkled in the mild sunlight and made him look even more handsome. The wind was so strong that it might have made Sarah fall down. So Aditya stood shielding her from the wind.

After some time…

'You look fabulous today' said Sarah.

Aditya smiled.

'Do you really love me?' asked Sarah thoughtfully.

'I do' replied Aditya.

'I still can't believe it. It just feels like one of my dreams. I'm scared that I would wake up tomorrow to find this all a dream.'

Aditya smiled at her and leaned close to her and look into her eyes. She looked innocently at him. He asked 'Do you trust me?'

'Yes.'

'Then trust me I do'

He sounded really serious that Sarah wasn't able to reply for a while. When she found her voice back, all that she could say was 'I… I love you too.'

Aditya leaned so close to her that she could feel his breath on her face.

Vrrrrrrrrroooooooooooooooom…..

It was a bike. This made them jump and they moved away from each other. As soon as the bike disappeared out of sight, Sarah put her hands on Aditya's collar and pulled him towards her. He gently kissed her soft lips. He did not know how many seconds flew past. That moment felt like an eternity. He didn't want to let go of her. She hugged him and he held her in his arms. It was the happiest moment in his life.

'Well… Do you still think this is a dream?' asked Aditya looking at Sarah who was holding his hands tightly.

'No! But it's just too good to be real!' replied Sarah.

She let him go when his mobile rang. It was a call from Sid. The movie had gotten over and he was coming back to pick them up. Though it took Sid and

Preethi half an hour to reach there it only seemed like seconds for Aditya. Time flew away like mad when he was with Sarah.

And he knew it deep in his heart that he couldn't survive without her.

*****

Chapter 10

In second year, Sarah became a paying guest at Preethi's home. She had often stayed there earlier and so she was well acquainted with Preethi's family. Aditya invited her for a live in and she said a sharp 'no'.

Aditya said Sarah was a 'Miss Perfect' because everything she did was too perfect and he often commented that she would use a scale and the geometry tools to arrange her books in a stack and even her plans for her future were perfect too. He slowly understood that besides being jovial and understanding she was very ambitious. Aditya can give her whatever money can buy but her desire was to be a step ahead of the others. She wanted Aditya to do his MBA in some better institute in India. He too agreed to do whatever she said if that made her happy.

This particular semester kept everyone busy. Though they met once in a week or so they didn't have much time to hang out together. The time went by without any significant event. Sarah was poring over her books since she was seriously insisted on giving a consistent performance in the semester exams by her parents and as usually Preethi was sleeping most of the time. No one has ever beaten Preethi in her record of having slept for nearly twenty hours a day. Sid and Aditya were busy with their robotics project. They were keen on making it to the IIT this time.

Two days into the semester exams...

Sarah was waiting for Aditya in the canteen. After about ten minutes Aditya came with a round of apologies for being late. 'Sorry Sorry…. I'm late' said Aditya.

'That's okay. I'm hungry. Let's get our lunch first' replied Sarah.

'Ok' said Aditya and went to the billing counter and after about another ten minutes came back with two plates of noodles.

Sarah took one of the plates and started eating. She was so hungry. After dumping a mouthful of noodles, she asked Aditya 'So?'

'What so?'

'You said you have news.'

'Yes. You are now the popular girlfriend of the secretary of the Robotics club. And my project goes to IIT Kharagpur this year.'

Sarah gaped at him unbelievably.

'Stop staring now' breathed Aditya.

'Oh! Sorry! But are you really telling me that you are going to IIT next month?' asked Sarah.

'Isn't that amazing?'

'Well… Wow! That's really cool! It was your hard work and you have achieved it. Congrats!' exclaimed the surprised Sarah.

'Thanks to you Sarah. It was all because of you I started going on' said Aditya looking at her.

'For God's sake, stop those old theories now. I did nothing. It's all your work' replied Sarah soothingly. She gets annoyed if Aditya started on old stories again.

'Ask me anything now. I'll get it for you!'

'Are you sure you can get anything for me?'

'Just ask me.'

After a moment's thought…

'Promise me to love me forever!'

Aditya said 'I solemnly swear that I will love Sarah and only Sarah till my last breath.'

Sarah smiled mischievously and said 'Let's see how long you keep up your promise.'

'I mean it Sarah. And you know it. Now stop insulting me.'

'Okay. Calm down. Now get me an ice cream.'

*****

Sarah was lying on her bed reading 'twilight' gifted to her by Aditya.

Sarah's croaky sang. She had changed her ring tone at last. It was a call from Aditya. She eagerly picked it up and said 'What's up Addie?'

Aditya asked 'Tomorrow is your last exam right?'

'Yep!'

'Can you wait near the cafeteria for me after your exam? I'll meet you there.'

'Yes. I'll wait. You could have texted me this.'

'I wanted to hear you talk. Don't act as if you are not pleased. And please stop calling me Addie. You know I hate that name.'

'Well… I am glad you called up, Addie.'

'Sarah!' exclaimed Aditya angrily.

'Ok ok cool down Aditya' said Sarah playfully.

'Ok then. We will meet tomorrow. And do your exam well.'

The line went dead.

*****

The next day when the exam got over Sarah walked straight to the café. She sat in a nearby chair and put her bag in the adjacent one and was watching the cars that were parked in the college. There was the usual row of a Toyota Innova, a Maruti Swift, a Ford, a Camry and a Hyundai. A few minutes passed by and a shiny black Skoda entered the campus. She has never seen it in the campus before and she was wondering who its owner would be. On a closer look she found the owner was none other than her own sweetheart Aditya. The car came to a halt in front of the cafeteria. Sarah walked to the car and Aditya opened the door for her.

'You never said you had a Skoda!' exclaimed Sarah as she got in.

'You never asked. So how was your exam?' replied Aditya and smiled his charming smile.

'I've done them well' said Sarah with a sigh and added 'Where are we going?'

'We will meet Sid at his house.'

'Why?'

'It's his birthday today.'

'Oh my God! I totally forgot. I don't have a gift now. Damn!'

'That's ok. We have a gift for him' said Aditya and jerked his thumb towards the rear seat.

'Well. What is it?'

'Secret!'

'Oh! C'mon Aditya. I hate secrets.'

Aditya switched on the car stereo which against its usual nature played a Taylor Swift song to make her shut up. It was always rock that Aditya liked which Sarah regarded only mad people like him and Sid listened to.

After sometime's thought Sarah said to Aditya 'I hate people who are richer than me Aditya. And you are definitely richer than me.'

'Why?' asked Aditya curiously.

'I have a million reasons.'

'Shoot it.'

'One: They are richer than me. Two: They keep changing their things for new ones- cars, houses, girlfriends etc. Three: They are filthy rich…'

'You're so prejudiced! I swear I won't change my car and my girlfriend. Both are too good.'

Sarah smiled and said in a complaining tone 'My mother is a surgeon and she saves lives. What do I do? Waste my mother's money.'

'That's silly. It applies to every kid. It's my dad who is rich. One day when I take up a business on my own I'll definitely be much better than I am now.'

'I want to earn a lot too.'

'At times you make me feel as if I'm talking to a highly ambitious school kid who never talks other stuff than her grades and how to improve them' said Aditya with a smile and added 'With all our theories on rich people I forgot to tell you the most important thing. We are meeting my mom at Sid's home. She wants to meet you too.'

'Aditya! You are a fraud! You forgot to tell me? Am I supposed to look like this when I meet your mom for the first time? Look! Half of my makeup is undone. My eyeliner has worn off. I can't come. Drive me home. I need to put on a better dress.'

'Hey! Trust me. You look as cute as ever.'

'You always say this even if I look like a half dead drug addict!' commented Sarah.

Sarah was fuming with anger. She checked herself in the car's rearview mirror and was trying to adjust her hair.

'I definitely look like a drug addict. Look at my eyes! The kaajal is smudged everywhere' cried Sarah.

'Oh Come on Sarah! If it's not today when will you meet her? She is very eager to meet you.'

'She knows me?'

'There was never a day spent without me mentioning your name to her over phone' replied Aditya and added soon as Sarah looked scared 'Don't panic. She knows you and Sid are my best friends. And Preethi too.'

'We could have brought Preethi too.'

'She will be there already. Sid picked her up from home.'

'So this was all planned by you three!'

'It took you this long to guess. Poor Sarah!' and added after a few seconds 'I wish I could take you on a long drive… alone.' Sarah blushed. She gave him a soft punch.

Sarah was actually happy that she was going to meet Aditya's mum. But she was in a total surprise when this had happened all of a sudden without any prior plans. She was silent throughout the rest of the travel and appeared to be deep in thought when their car crossed the Anna Nagar traffic signal and they entered the Anna arch. Her heart was beating faster than it would have if she had met Aditya in an empty lane on a cold night.

After about five minutes or so Aditya drove the car inside the gates of Sid's house in Anna nagar and brought it to a halt in front of it. Out of the corner of her eyes Sarah had been watching him drive. Sarah was about to get out of the car when Aditya said 'Wait!'

'Why?' asked Sarah and looked at him puzzled.

She could hear Preethi's voice announcing their arrival. Preethi appeared at the doorway immediately and she was holding the door eagerly open for them. Aditya got out of the car first and came to Sarah's side and opened the door for her and held out a hand to her. She smiled and got out of the car holding his hand.

Preethi commented 'You two are just too much. You live in the twenty first century Chennai. This is not the classical England.'

Aditya closed the door behind them as the girls entered the hall. 'Both the mums are busy in the kitchen. Sid just went somewhere. Let's enter the forbidden kingdom. Come' said Preethi to Sarah updating her about everything that had happened before she arrived.

'The kitchen?' asked Sarah.

'Yes'

Aditya followed the girls to the kitchen upstairs. There were two women who were almost of the same height; both looked beautiful for their age. One of them was busy chopping the onions and the other was stirring the stew. Sarah at once recognized Aditya's mum as the one who was chopping onions as he had taken after his mum. His mother was really beautiful. The beauty of her youth still remained with her and it reminded her of her mum.

'Mom!' called Aditya. Both the women looked up and Aditya took Sarah to the one who was chopping onions. 'This is Sarah!' he introduced. And to Sarah 'My mom!'

'Oh Sarah! How do you do?' asked Aditya's mum and gave her a hug and a kiss on her forehead. The fear in Sarah's mind had vanished at once. She began to like her at once.

'Fine. Thank you!' replied Sarah politely.

Sid's mother came around after reducing the flame in the stove and said 'Our Sid once told me about your hostel adventures and why the girls of his class never liked the two of you. You had your exam today?'

'Yes. It was just Oops.'

'Oops?' asked Sid's mom.

'Object oriented programming! We call it oops' replied Sarah with a smile.

'I've heard you are good in nick naming stuff' said Aditya's mum and added 'How did you do your exams?' and exactly at that moment Sid entered the room and said 'She is gonna run away now. Let her relax before you shoot her with your questions.'

'Happy birthday Sid!' called out Sarah and rushed to give him a hug.

'Thanks' said Sid who was about to go downstairs after Aditya and added 'Come down soon after your interview Sarah. We'll watch a video together. It really helps feeling better after writing exams.' Sarah smiled and nodded. The girls stayed in the kitchen to help.

'Fetch her some juice Preethi!' said Sid's mum to Preethi. Sarah was sitting in a chair next to Aditya's mother. Preethi poured the juice out of a large jug from the fridge into a tall glass and handed it to Sarah. Then she went to stir the stew to help Sid's mum. She had taken a liking to Sid's mum because she constantly made fun of her son and told her how she would be glad to switch kids with Preethi's mum. Sarah sat sipping the water melon juice and when Aditya's mum occasionally asked about her course and studies she gave her a very big account about it. Sarah enjoyed talking and Aditya's mom was pleased with her detailed stories. Preethi got bored and left downstairs to see what the guys were up to.

In a few minutes the song 'boulevard of broken dreams' was deafeningly played from downstairs. Both the mums got irritated with the noise. Sarah went near the staircase and shouted 'Guys! Keep the volume down!' And the sound went down a few decibels.

'These kids are always like this!' smiled Aditya's mum to Sarah.

'I have told my Sid that he is gonna become totally deaf in a year or so. I don't understand how they like this. But I like them both in action with their guitar and drums.'

'Yeah! They were awesome in the cultural fest when I was in my first year' said Sarah.

After a detailed account about college life…

'Well…Sarah. I wanted to ask you something. Is Priya getting married?'

'Aditya told me so' replied Sarah. This was the shortest answer she had said in almost an hour. Sarah was scared to talk about Priya. She didn't want to give away the unpleasant details but somehow she felt that Aditya's mother would have known everything that her son had done. Because after all she is his mother. Her eyes said it all. And what she said next proved it.

'Aditya had a crush on her. I've never seen him talk about anyone like that before. He hated college until he found her. I know he hid a lot of things from me. He didn't want me to suffer. He didn't allow me to come to see him. He told me not to waste my time on him. I just want him to finish his studies without any complications. You friends have to tell him. He won't listen to me and his dad. He will shout and never talk for a week if I advise him.'

Sarah smiled at her and said 'Yes aunty! We friends will tell him.'

At that moment three voices called out in chorus from downstairs, 'Sarah!'

Aditya's mum said 'You go and join them or they will come here to rescue you.'

Sarah smiled and went down to join them.

She went to the living room where the trio sat watching the movie 'Terminator 2'. She moved to the middle of the room and stood there with her hands over her hips and glared at the three of them. The three craned their necks and ignored her. Aditya said 'Out of the way Little Miss! You are blocking the TV.'

'What were you guys thinking…planning behind my back?' asked Sarah.

'Actually we did it right under your nose' giggled Preethi.

As Sarah tried to hit Preethi with a cushion which she caught and redirected it back to Sarah whom Aditya shielded from getting hit and forced her to get seated.

'Pack of mad people' muttered Sarah.

'Except me' said Sid.

The four of them watched the movie and after Sid's dad came they had dinner together. That was the best dinner the four had together. Sid didn't like the idea of cutting cakes. He said that only kids did that and that he was twenty one. So on his behalf Sarah and Preethi cut the cake. It was a black forest and they fought over it. Sid had agreed to celebrate it only for the reason that they four could be together over dinner at his home.

Usually it was Aditya who would have eaten half of what was kept in Sarah's plate but today since his mum was with them she had to eat it fully herself.

When dessert was served, Sid announced 'I want you guys to come with me to my cousin's wedding reception held in a resort in the ECR (East Coast Road). It's exclusively for friends and some very close relatives.'

'Sid! Rishabd's wedding reception?' asked Sid's dad raising an eyebrow on his son.

'Yeah! He invited me for the reception and asked me to bring my friends too. Even my school pals are coming' and added to the others 'So…Are you in?'

'We can't come' whined Sarah and Preethi together.

'Why?' asked Sid.

'My mom won't allow me if Sarah doesn't come' replied Preethi.

'Well... I'm going to my home town. It has been so long you know. I need a break' replied Sarah.

'Sarah! It's just two days. We won't get another chance. Please do come' pleaded Sid.

She looked at Aditya for help but he too wanted her to come. So finally she said 'I will come if my mum says yes'.

'When's the reception?' asked Preethi.

'On Christmas eve' replied Sid.

'Christmas Eve again!' teased Preethi now looking at Sarah and Aditya.

Sarah glared at her so she kept quiet.

'What is so unusual about Christmas eve?' asked Aditya's mum looking curious.

'Well. It has been a year since we have dumped an ice cream on Preethi's face' said Sid and added to Preethi 'How about one this year too?'

For this Sid's mum's disapproving tone called 'Sid!'

'Oh! Sorry mom! I forgot you were listening.'

'I'll talk to your parents if you want me to', offered Sid's mom to Sarah and Preethi.

'Thanks moms!' exclaimed Sid gleefully.

The girls too thanked her.

The dinner got over with more plans about their upcoming visit to the resort in ECR. Sid's parents and Aditya's mum were really happy to see them all together.

Sarah and Preethi were given a hug by Aditya's mum before they bid good bye. 'Take care Sarah! And you Preethi!' she said.

'Preethi! Do visit us often dear!' said Sid's mum. 'It would be lovely to have you here.'

Sid drove the girls home since Aditya had to take his mum home. Though Sarah had secretly wished that Aditya would take them back she perfectly understood the situation. It was one of the greatest days in her life. Her heart had hammered like mad when Aditya told her about her impending meeting with his mum. But she had instantly liked his mum the moment she saw her. Something about her reminded her of her own mum. Maybe all the mothers in the world were so sweet.

When Aditya phoned her that night, she said 'I like your mum more than I like you. She is so sweet.'

'I know that. That's why I wanted you to meet her.'

'But you really caught me offhand today. But still I forgive you … Anything for your mum.'

'She likes you too. She filled me with theories of Sarah all the way home. Now you sleep. You must be really tired. I will call you tomorrow. Good night!'

'Goodnight Aditya! Love you!'

*****

Chapter 11

The fine day had actually left an imprint by turning the evening so pleasant and the added pleasure was that it was also the Christmas Eve of the year. The grand hall had been decorated in colorful drapes and beautiful white flowers stood in large vases near the decorated hallway. Two human sized statues of fairies were placed one on either side of the doorway. It was like some ancient Greek house. The dance floor had been occupied by the angel like bride and the handsome groom. Small round tables with light colored table clothes were arranged beautifully in order in the hall. The hall was dimly lit and candlelight filled the room kindling a romantic effect. The place smelt of fresh roses and other flowers.

The party was about to begin and it would definitely last for hours on end. Since it was exclusively for friends alone and very dear family friends, there was dance and song of the kind for which most parents would raise an eyebrow. Well it doesn't mean that the party was raucous, it was pretty well decent. Here in Tamilnadu this was quite unusual... all these dancing and singing.

The band began to play and the newly wed couple was swaying to the tunes like two beautiful stars. They looked so elegant on the dance floor. Soon everyone joined them waltzing on the dance floor.

Sarah was dressed in a pretty blue designer salwar which Aditya had selected for her and was waiting for him to join her. Preethi looked pretty in an orange outfit. She was having a great time of her life and was commenting about every guy her eyes met.

'My wedding will be totally a traditional one. My mom is pretty serious about that. I won't have a chance to shake a leg then' Preethi said and let out a sigh.

'Don't worry Preethi. You will have a chance in my wedding. Wedding in a church in Goa and the reception in some better place than this. What do you think?' asked Sarah.

'Sounds good. Aditya will be pleased. Well... Let me fetch a drink for us' said Preethi and disappeared into the crowd.

Sarah had been waiting so long for Aditya and she was beginning to lose patience. She looked around and found that almost every table was full of folks chatting and laughing away. She began missing Aditya. She took out her croaky to call him and exactly at that moment Preethi returned back with drinks for them, her face was wearing an expression

'Intolerable'. Sarah could see that she was bursting with news.

'What happened?' enquired Sarah.

'Where is Aditya now?' asked Preethi.

'Probably with Sid! They went out to get something.'

'Very well. You are wrong. Just turn around and have a look at the dance floor. He is dancing with that female Sanjana who has been trying to woo him from yesterday evening.'

'You saw him?'

'Well… I suppose he was coming to meet you and on the way she asked him to dance with her and he went. I reckon she is trying to impress him. Terrible flirt!'

Sarah was definitely angry and she went almost red but she tried to conceal her anger in front of Preethi. A bitter pang of jealousy surged through her.

'How dare he make me wait for him while he is dancing away with some stupid girl?' thought Sarah but she didn't voice it.

She turned and looked past a couple of tables to have a better view at the dance floor. There he was… Aditya, the guy she loved and for whom she had come there, dancing with Sanjana. She couldn't tolerate it. She got up from her chair and walked past the dancing couples, for the first time in her life not banging into anything even in her hurry and finally approached Aditya in the dance floor. He stopped dancing when he saw her coming and smiled at her… his usual charming smile.

'Shall we dance?' he asked Sarah offering her his hand.

'I was waiting for you all this time but you...' said Sarah angrily to Aditya pointing to Sanjana and added 'I'm leaving this place this very moment. I came to say good bye, Aditya!' Sarah angrily retorted.

'Shh! Wait a sec!' said Aditya giving her a gentle tap on her lips with his finger and disappeared from the dance floor leaving Sarah in the company of Sanjana. She tried not to look at her and so she walked slowly back to the table. Preethi saw her coming and said 'Where did you suddenly disappear into?' Sarah sat down without replying. Preethi exclaimed pointing to the band 'Hey look!'

Sarah turned around immediately and looked back. She saw Aditya on the stage. He was holding the mike and said 'This song is for everyone present here and for the couple of the night, the lovely bride and the handsome groom.' Sarah remembered how she had admired his voice during the college cultural fest and her anger suddenly vanished like a wisp of smoke. She felt like grinning but hid it though the edges of her lips gave it up.

Aditya began to play the guitar and soon Sarah realized that it was the Bryan Adams' song 'Everything I do, I do it for you'. Of course the song did its magic. Everyone on the dance floor paired up, eyes met, and the spirit was high and love was in the air all of a sudden. For a few minutes the place had been filled with Aditya's enchanting voice that covered the entire place with a romantic ambience.

Finally Aditya ended the song with 'Everything I do I do it for you, Sarah' resulting in a round of applause...

Suddenly Sarah felt all the eyes upon her. She had gone very pink. This time she was blushing... not angry. Her cheeks were burning. She felt breathless. She rushed out of the room to get some air and stood out in the balcony facing the sea. The potted plants were arranged neatly in the balcony and hanging plants were hung at regular intervals. The night sea breeze was very cold in that month of the year and she felt the chillness tickling her. Aditya followed her out moments later, went near her and held her hand with a firmness that she had always loved.

He said 'So... you win.'

'What?' asked Sarah puzzled.

'Well... Just now you made a rocker sing a romantic song for you in front of an entire hall of audience.'

'Oh! That... was pretty good' said Sarah suppressing her laughter.

The party was in full swing as they began to walk towards the beach hand in hand away from the noise and cacophony of the hall towards the tranquility and calm symphony of the cool breeze with the waves of the ocean breaking in and out of the welcoming arms of the shore.

Aditya took off his blazer and put it around Sarah who was nearly shivering in the cold breeze.

Just then she pulled Aditya by his collar and kissed his lips. He wasn't surprised. As he knew Sarah very well, he had been expecting this to happen. She looked into his eyes and said 'Possessiveness and all these… I can't help it Aditya.'

'Scared that I'll leave you? I won't' said Aditya and gave her cheek a little peck.

They were looking at each other for a moment in silence when headlights flashed blindingly into their eyes. Aditya pulled Sarah out of the way immediately and shielded her. It was a Land Rover and it came to a halt just inches away from them.

Someone got out of the Land Rover laughing. It was Sid and one of Aditya's cousins. 'Scared you guys!' exclaimed Sid.

'Well… That was close to murder, Sid. Driving like mad!' said Aditya to Sid.

'Look who's talking about mad driving!' exclaimed Sid and added 'We have planned an overnight party. So went to get some aspirin just in case anyone had a hangover. Wanna join us?' asked Sid.

'No' said Aditya immediately before Sarah could nudge him in his ribs.

'That's ok. I'll be late' said Sid and added 'You've got our room key right?'

'Yep' replied Aditya.

'Keep the car keys with you too' said Sid and threw it to Aditya who caught it. Sarah was admiring his every move like an ardent tennis fan would do on seeing each stroke made by some legendary player.

'We are going inside. You guys go for a ride. It's really nice out there' said Sid.

'Carry on guys! Bye!' said Sarah.

'Bye!' said Sid and commented 'Whoa! Someone's getting laid tonight!'

'Shut up you git!' said Aditya and gave a punch on Sid's shoulder. The guys left. Sarah and Aditya got into the car.

As soon as Sarah got into the car she was amused by its smell. 'Hmm… The car smells good. It smells like a flower garden.'

'They brought the bouquets of flower for decorations in this car this afternoon' replied Aditya and added 'You like it?'

She nodded in reply.

Aditya revved up the car and they began their long drive after a long time together. Into the welcoming arms of the dark night, the stars shining on an almost moonless sky drove Aditya and Sarah together. Sarah had forgotten how long it had been since their last drive together.

*****

The sky was clear that night and the moon looked the size of a finger nail. Millions of stars were shining like diamonds sparkling in a pitch black party wear designed by some popular designer for a Hollywood actress going to some film festival.

The Land Rover was parked at a reasonable distance from the sea. The cool sea breeze was playing gently over Sarah's face; her silky hair was brushed against her face by the wind. She had snuggled close to Aditya resting her head on his chest. She could actually feel his heart beat. The sound of the waves mixed with that of the breeze brought together an almost heavenly rhythm.

'Sarah! You bring an aura of happiness wherever you go' said Aditya.

'Do I?' asked Sarah.

'Yes, you don't have any idea about how special you are to me.'

Sarah simply smiled.

'Do you love me Sarah?'

'Yes… But less than globe trotting!' said Sarah smiling playfully.

'Globe trotting?' asked Aditya surprised.

'Yeah! I feel like I want to talk. Shall I say something? But it's definitely gonna be big. You have to bear with me' Sarah started in a playful tone.

'Have I ever refused?'

'Well. Did you know I liked you before we were even friends?'

'Yes. You girls used to turn up everywhere Sid and I went. I didn't mind it much though my class girls saw to it right? Were you stalking me? I thought you were Sid's fans.'

'No. I found you and Sid really amazing. The moment I saw you... Maybe it'll sound like some stupid movie or some crap novel but the truth is I knew something was gonna happen between us. But then I came to know about Priya. So I just kept quiet and you know what… the times we four spent together I would secretly be admiring you. Sid caught me in this act once and told me not to waste my time on you. I lied to him it was just a crush. And when you proposed I was really shocked. It came down on me so suddenly because at that time I was actually struggling with my conscience that you were just a friend and all that. But I never thought you would love me. Even now I can't believe it…. I have always wanted to ask you one thing. Do you still love Priya?'

There was a moment's silence.

'I don't understand from where you stir up such curious questions. I was ready to die for her but I wanted to live for you. It's you I love. Trust me. I will never leave you' replied Aditya stroking her cheeks thoughtfully.

'I have always had a feeling that I don't deserve to be loved by you. Do you really love me?'

'Yes'

'How much?'

'More than life' said Aditya and gave her a hug.

'You know Sarah! I thought I could never love again. It was really hard to believe that you loved me. I felt unworthy of your love. You made me realize what life is all about' said Aditya now stroking Sarah's head and gave her a kiss on her forehead.

Sarah could feel his breath on her hair. She said 'You are just twenty one. You speak as if you are a philosopher or something of a century's worth experience. Are you drunk?' wondered Sarah not expecting any reply from him.

'Someone called Sarah the philosopher told me "My love is like a phoenix bird born out of ashes of a dead love" and she calls me a philosopher' said Aditya and added 'Not fair Sarah.'

Two minutes flew past...

Sarah pointed to the sky and said 'You see those stars? That's us.'

'Which ones?' asked Aditya following where Sarah was pointing.

Sarah said 'The Triangulum Australe. The left one's you and the middle one's me.'

'What about the right one then?' asked Aditya.

'We'll give it to Sid if he wants and let the fourth one be Preethi or else she'll feel bad too' replied Sarah in a sleepy tone and pulled herself closer to Aditya.

Aditya hugged her close and said with a smile 'You're a crazy little kid Sarah! You always talk like mad.'

Sarah didn't say anything back. She was thinking. How true the words are? How Aditya and Sarah had become a living example for those words?

There wasn't much time for more words as they had to go back to the party and they had to return home the next day. And Preethi must be wondering where they were. Sarah fell asleep resting on Aditya's chest cuddled close to him. The next day everyone will be returning back to the hustle and bustle of reality and who knows there will be no time to love.

Chapter 12

The fourth semester came to an end as fast as it had begun. For Sarah the practical exams were going on.

Sarah was quite serious when it came to studies and exams.

'Please God! Let it not be the sorting program' prayed Sarah as she took her question paper in the Data Structures laboratory.

She turned the paper around.

'Heap sort!' groaned Sarah. The earth seemed to slip away from under her legs. Her knees felt wobbly as if she was standing in knee deep water. She got fully tensed that she didn't know what to do next. She went to her seat and sat there totally upset with her hands over her face. Tears trickled down her fingers. Seconds ticked past.

After about five minutes or so she wiped her face with her hand towel and said to herself 'Relax! Calm down. See what can be done now. Stop behaving like a silly stupid school girl!'

She exchanged the question for which fifteen marks were deducted. That exam became a nightmare for her. She went to the café and sat there alone. No Preethi. No Sid. And especially no Aditya. She was happy they were not there. She hated crying in their presence. They'll tease her.

She was in an awful mood the next two days. Preethi knew it and she kept quiet as she didn't want to become the victim of Sarah's anger. She had a fight with Aditya for he had been busy and hadn't picked up the phone when she had called. Now she was angry that he hadn't called her back to convince her even. That was so like Aditya. He always left her alone whenever she was upset saying that he would talk when she is back to normal. Sarah hated this as she expected him to say something to console her.

Sarah was reading something from the twilight saga and it was raining outside. She loved this weather and the book created a good effect on her. She missed Aditya. When she began to search for her phone to call him, her phone rang. Call from Aditya. She was really glad that he called.

'Hello' she said.

'Still angry?' asked Aditya.

'A little...but with myself. Aditya, I almost flunked in the lab exam. I feel so miserable.'

'That's ok Sarah! You can compensate in the theory exams if you do them better. And I'm sure you will do them really well, won't you?'

'Yes' said Sarah feeling better.

'So this was the thing bothering you so badly for the past two days eh?'

'Yes'

'I have grand news for you' announced Aditya.

'What is it?'

'Well. I have got admission for MBA in Australia'

'Australia? I thought you were gonna try for the IIMs.'

'Well... I wanted to give you a surprise. Aren't you happy?'

She didn't reply.

'Hey! What happened?' asked Aditya.

'Nothing... You could have told me before Aditya. You know I hate secrets. And I'll miss you badly.'

'I'll miss you too. Are you ok? Do you want me to come?'

'No. I am fine. I'll talk to you later.'

She cut the call.

She almost collapsed into a chair nearby.

Thoughts were circling her mind.

Deadly thoughts.

Venomous thoughts.

Thoughts that ruined the best moments of her life.

'What have I been doing? Two years of college life... Gone like smoke. Everyone is doing something worthy but look at me... I almost failed an exam. Well... he is not the reason. I am to be blamed. Not him. But he could have told me he was planning to go abroad. Anyway he is happy thinking that I am happy. Why should I spoil it? But I am hurt. Two years. I never gave this a thought that he'll be gone when I was still in college. It had never occurred to me. I was busy in love so I didn't think. But I will miss him a lot' wrote Sarah in her diary.

If Sarah could ever get irritated, it was only because of her thoughts. She had a habit of writing whatever she felt in her diary. She had a problem of expressing things she felt. Whatever she felt in her heart she can only write it and she can't speak it out. She had become very forgetful lately that she often forgot where she kept her diary. Or it must be Preethi who would have misplaced it along with her stuff. For complete two days it would go missing and then she would find it the next day right in front of her dresser or under the bed or beside the table lamp or along with the pile of laundry. Only Aditya had been successful enough to read her mind even if he was miles away from her. So she had never had to put efforts to explain stuff to him. And that is why she loved him a lot.

'Thoughts! Please go away! I am just confused!' wrote Sarah and closed her diary.

***

There was a deep silence in Preethi's room except for the CD player singing 'Forever and Always'. It was the most painful silence Preethi had ever seen. She had never seen Sarah like this. Preethi had nicknamed Sarah as 'Bubbly' as she was capable of changing any situation cheerful but now look at her. On seeing her, Preethi felt like crying and she was a novice in consoling people. It was usually done by Sarah. Sarah was sitting on Preethi's bed with her back to the wall. She had a pillow over her lap on which a book was kept open. She had been pretending to be reading but her eyes were fixed on a word and tears were falling from her eyes on to the book. She wiped it quickly so that Preethi would not notice.

'Sarah!' called Preethi and Sarah looked up.

'Stop crying now. Everything will be fine by morning. Stop imagining stuff' added Preethi.

'I am fine Preethi. I am just a bit upset.'

'You should be proud idiot. Stop being a cry baby. He told me if it hadn't been for you he wouldn't have got this scholarship. He does everything for you.'

'That's the problem Preethi. You won't understand. He does everything for me even if I don't want it. He says he wants me to be happy. Why the hell does he care?' shouted Sarah.

'You don't want him to go to Australia?'

'It's not that. Though I will miss him I want him to go. It's his life, his studies, his career. I won't stop him.'

'Then what?' asked Preethi.

After a few seconds Sarah narrated her tale.

*****

Sarah had just had her GRE classes and she was on her way back home. She went to the juice shop which she usually visited and to her surprise…

'Sid! Aditya! What are you doing here?' exclaimed Sarah.

'Obviously... having a juice' said Sid and raised the tall juice glass in his hand. Sarah took a seat beside him.

'We had some work nearby. So we thought we could meet you on the way' said Aditya.

'Congratulations!' said Sarah as she extended her hand and shook hands with Aditya.

'Don't you think you are being so formal with me?' asked Aditya.

'Am I? Do you expect me to hug and kiss you in front of everyone then?' asked Sarah and shrugged her shoulders. Aditya placed an order for a water melon juice for Sarah. Sid's mobile rang and he went out to talk. Aditya began the conversation.

'Listen Sarah! This is important. I'll be leaving in a month. Now look... Stop looking pathetic. I don't know how to tell this but... I'm really sorry!' his tone was indeed serious.

'Sorry for what?' exclaimed Sarah.

'I am sorry that I have been disturbing you a lot.'

'No. You are not.'

'Wait! Listen to me. I love you and always will...'

'Yes. But...'

'I know you love me too. But Sarah I just realized it's not your fault that you fell in love with me.'

'Stop it Aditya! For God's sake tell me what is happening?'

'I just don't want to ruin your life. You are an ambitious girl. You have helped me a lot through hard times, brought myself back to me. I care for you Sarah. There is a long way to go in life. I guess this is not the right time for you to have fallen in love with me.'

'You are talking like mad Aditya! And it's already too late to realize that!' exclaimed Sarah and laughed at him.

'I don't know Sarah. I might become a reason someday for certain good things that never happened to you. And two years... Who knows what will happen?' said Aditya. Sarah was getting irritated.

'Good things like what? I am in no mood to play games now' replied an irritated Sarah.

'Well... Look. Just imagine... Two years. And you have a lot of dreams to chase right?'

'Yes' replied Sarah.

'Ok then. Let's be a bit practical. Being in love will definitely make you think about me and it will distract you a lot. All the time you go out or do something, you will want to talk to me or text me. What would you have done if we hadn't met at all?'

Sarah thought for a while and said smirking 'Do you think I would have gone dating Arjun?'

'Who's Arjun?' asked Aditya curiously.

'My classmate, he's brainy.'

'Well Sarah, Stop kidding now! Life will always not be like the stupid novels you read. Do you get that?' asked Aditya.

Sarah nodded.

Aditya took her hand in his and said 'I guess the only solution for this is…' He hesitated for a moment and said '… why don't we take a break?'

'Trust me. I still love you and I do care for you. We will be friends for the next two years and let's see what happens. What do you say?' added Aditya immediately as Sarah looked so horribly confused.

Sarah now understood what he had been trying to say. She asked 'What? Are you trying to say that I might fall for someone else in two years? If yes, you are mistaken. Completely!' and added 'If you really think we need a break then do as you wish Aditya!'

'And it's getting really late. I must be going' said Sarah, picked her bag up and left the place angrily. Aditya was looking at her going away from him. His heart ached to see her going away. 'I don't know how I'm going to breathe without her around me!' wondered Aditya. Sid was standing at the doorway looking puzzled.

*****

'Is that all Sarah? You scared me. I thought you guys had a real break up. A real one you know. Silly' said Preethi bursting into laughter and added 'You have a wide imagination Sarah! He will definitely call you. Sid told me that he can't stay for an hour without at least texting you.'

'Oh! That's why he hadn't called me even once in two days?'

'Oops. Maybe he is busy…'

Before Preethi could complete her sentence her phone rang. It was Aditya.

'Hello Aditya!'

'Hi Preethi! Is Sarah there?' asked Aditya on the other end.

'Yes. Any problem?'

'No. I tried calling her but she is not answering my call for the past two days. I don't know what's wrong with her.'

'She's just upset. Talk to her' said Preethi and handed the phone to Sarah and called her a 'Fraud'.

Sarah took the phone and said, 'Sorry Aditya! I was angry and I am still angry.'

'Hey! I am sorry too. I was upset. That's why I spoke like mad. Should I really go Sarah?' asked Aditya.

'I think yes. You should go.'

'Well. I am leaving next month. I'll be going back to Mumbai in a week. I'll meet you in college before I leave. I am really busy these days. I hope you understand.'

'Yes Aditya! I know. Take care. Stay in touch, won't you?'

'I will, sweetheart. I love you!' His voice showed pain and it immediately brought tears in Sarah's eyes.

'I love you too. Looking forward to see you. Bye!'

*****

It was a Friday evening. Preethi and Sarah were waiting near the reception of the college for Aditya.

He had told them that he would meet them there. And they had exactly fifteen minutes before the buses start from the college. Sarah was growing restless and was looking at her watch every five seconds. And there he was… Aditya, looking cool as usual walking towards them. Sarah felt like running into his arms immediately but then with great efforts she restrained herself from doing so.

'Hey galz!' said Aditya.

'The college buses will leave in ten minutes Aditya. You are late. I should leave soon' replied Sarah.

'Look! Isn't that Priya?' exclaimed Aditya pointing to a girl standing some ten feet away. And of course that was Priya.

'Wait here Sarah. I'll be back in a minute' said Aditya and left to meet Priya before Sarah could utter anything. She looked blankly at Preethi who returned a sheepish smile not knowing what to do.

'Hey Priya!' called Aditya as he walked towards Priya. She smiled and waved her hand back. She looked quite different from the Priya that these people knew. She was no more wearing those bright salwars. She had finally learnt what colors suited her. And she had had a haircut. No more long plaited hair.

'How are you?' asked Priya to Aditya.

'Great actually!' replied Aditya and added 'Well… I'm leaving to Mumbai this Sunday. I've got admission for MBA in Australia. I'm leaving next month.'

'Wow! That's really a good thing Aditya. And the Robotics club did really well this year. So finally you made it to the IIT symposium this year!' said Priya.

'Well… Without Sid and Sarah I couldn't have done it.'

Six minutes to go.

Five minutes.

Four.

Preethi and Sarah got restless and Sarah called out 'Aditya!' and showed her watch.

Aditya said 'Just a minute Sarah!' and he happily continued chatting with Priya.

Three minutes.

Two.

Preethi got very angry. She beckoned Sarah to follow her to the bus. Sarah was very much irritated and so she left without even bidding bye to Aditya.

One minute.

Aditya bid goodbye to Priya at last and turned to go back to Sarah. But she was nowhere to be found. He looked at his watch and cursed himself as the college buses started to leave the campus. Sarah was too angry to speak and so she didn't pick her phone when Aditya called. She could get angry quite easily. She opened a novel and tried reading it but it didn't help. So she kept down the book, closed her eyes and said to herself with gritted teeth 'Calm down Sarah! It's nothing'. She didn't utter a word to Preethi till they reached home.

*****

The Chennai Central…

The Central Railway station is the most crowded and the busiest place in Chennai. It was about seven in the evening and the place was buzzing with activity. At the entrance the police were checking every passenger's luggage. Inside, the display board was updating the arrival and departure of various trains in different platforms.

The entrance had a high level of security that day. The police were very alert and active. A Punjabi family was chattering away about something as they entered. The waiting room was almost full. Well… It was almost vacation for schools and that was the reason for the overwhelming crowd.

Aditya was standing in the Marry Brown counter buying a burger. He put the empty Styrofoam cup of Pepsi into the trash bin and took a look around. The shop that suddenly hit his eyes was 'Higginbothams', the book shop. Sarah would definitely have thrown a tantrum to buy her a book if she had been here. The thought of Sarah made Aditya miss her. He didn't know why he was doing it but he soon found himself walking towards 'Higginbotham's'. He entered the shop and looked around. There was this usual collection of Enid Blyton's children's stories, colorful comics like Archie, novels of famous authors like Sidney Sheldon, Danielle Steel, Nicholas Sparks and there was also our Chetan Bhagat's books. Aditya was least interested in books of fiction. He liked reality and he didn't like wasting time in folks and fiction. Sarah was exactly the opposite. He was scanning a particular group of books placed under classics and there was the usual collection of Cervantes, Shakespeare and Jane Austen.

There was a particular book in the classics shelf that caught his eyes. The book was maroon colored and it was hard bound with silver lettering on the outside. He took the book from its shelf and it was nothing but Jane Austen's 'Pride and Prejudice'. Aditya was never interested in such books but this one kindled his curiosity as Sarah had kept on mentioning this one. Aditya went to the counter with the book and paid for it. He packed the book inside his bag and decided to read it during the train journey.

He was walking towards the platform seven where he could wait till the train would arrive. Three girls who were standing near a Nescafe counter giggled as Aditya crossed them. A curious looking boy of about three years was running here and there on the platform, his dad caught him quickly and carried him away.

Aditya was totally stressed out after having written his GMAT exam. He had done it really well but he had wanted to stay in India but it was his father's idea that his son go abroad. Aditya's father had heard about Aditya's college tales and he had been freaking out saying that his son would go insane if he stayed there much longer. Aditya and his dad had quite a long argument about this and as usually his father had won. So he had no other options. He told his dad about Sarah and how important she was to him when his father was back from Dubai last month. His father and mother had gone there on a business trip.

Regarding Sarah, Aditya's father had just said 'You have time for everything later. Now for this moment's sake forget the girl. It's me who is earning for you and your mom. You are not old enough to get into relationships as strong as this.'

'Dad! I'm not asking you to permit me to marry her right now. I am just saying India has good business schools too. So why can't I do my MBA here?'

'When I was your age no one was there to send me abroad for studies. And now when you people have every opportunity to get quality education you are not willing to go. You can learn something you can't learn here Aditya. Life is not always easy. It's not just about chasing your love and achieving it. There are much more to life. I'm not asking you to totally let go of Sarah. Just two years. And who knows what can happen in two years.'

'I'll still love her.'

'Oh! Let's see!' replied his dad.

'Dad! If she had not stood by me during those days in college, I wouldn't be standing in front of you right now arguing about all this. I owe my life to her.'

'I understand Aditya but it doesn't change my decision to send you abroad. I want you to go. It's a deal. Do this for me and I won't stop your decisions after two years. I'm sure you'll be mature enough to think what is good for everyone after two years.'

'Well… If you think this is the best decision, I won't oppose you but promise me that you won't reject her once I come back after my post graduation.'

'Look! I'm not going to reject anything or anyone you consider important. But let's see who is going to reject what. I heard from your mom that she is a nice girl…that Sarah. But then it was the same with Priya wasn't it?' asked Aditya's dad.

Aditya's dad had obviously crossed the tolerance level of Aditya's temper. 'That's enough, Dad! Shut the hell up!' choked Aditya unable to control his overflowing emotions and he went out of the house. He wandered in the beach for a long time his mind going through the last sentence his Dad had said. He felt very much hurt.

*****

Aditya sat in a bench in platform seven that was quite clean and looked at his watch. It was eight o' clock and he had still one more hour to go. He was thinking about how best to kill the time left when he heard…

'Aditya!' called the sweetest voice on Earth and someone ran into his arms.

Aditya was actually surprised.

'Sarah! How did you come here?' asked Aditya giving her a tight hug.

'I just wanted to see you before you left. Sid brought me here. I'll miss you terribly!' said Sarah in a choked voice and tears were streaming down her eyes.

'Stop crying now. I don't want to remember you like this. I can't stand you crying. Please!' begged Aditya.

He wiped the tears off her eyes. She looked pathetic. But the anger she had possessed the day Priya had come had not vanished yet. Sid and Preethi came walking towards them. Sid gave Aditya a hug and said 'I'll miss you dude!'

'Me too!' replied Aditya.

'But then Aditya, you were so stupid to waste all the time we had together with Priya that day' said Sarah reminding him of his meeting with Priya.

'It has been long since I've met her. Busy with project I guess! I just wanted to tell her I'm leaving.'

'But what's the point Aditya?'

'I'm not mean like her. I still consider her a friend.'

'But she threw you away like trash. Remember?'

'I just don't want to do the same to her.'

'Aditya! You are supposed to ignore her and show her your attitude. Now that she's trying to get back into your life, are you telling me you're gonna forget whatever she did and that you're gonna accept her back?'

'Stop being a kid Sarah! No one is trying to make a comeback in my life. But I'm sure she can be my friend.'

'No Aditya. That's not possible. After all the efforts we put... I put to make you go on, you can't just go ahead and take her into your life as anything.'

'Don't talk like mad Sarah. Don't you trust me?'

'It's not about trust Aditya! Have I ever asked you anything serious before? I'm just scared for you. It's possible she can hurt you again and I don't want that to happen. Please Aditya! Stay away from her. Did she brainwash you now?'

'Gosh! How wide your imagination goes? Sarah!' wondered Aditya and added to Sid 'Sid! Talk some sense into her!'

Sid asked 'What are you guys going off about? You spoke with Priya? If you want my opinion about Priya you know very well what I would say, Aditya. Stay away. If you want her then you can very well forget us all.'

'Sid! Try to understand. It won't be the same as before. I just thought it would be good to be her friend rather than being an ex boyfriend. I won't get hurt anyway.'

'Yes! You are right Aditya. You won't get hurt. You'll hurt us all instead. You'll do this all for someone who doesn't mean anything to you at all' replied Sarah curtly.

'This is how you have understood me Sarah! I'm upset' said Aditya angrily.

'Well... I'm the one who makes you upset!' cried Sarah her eyes revealing tears.

'Yes. You are a great pain. And you know what, you spoilt my mood and so goes the entire day. Thanks for everything Sarah!' said Aditya through gritted teeth.

Sarah stood dumbfound with shock seeing that it had been Aditya who had uttered all these words of pure hatred. Sid was unable to find words.

'Aditya! No one has ever spoken to me like this. Not even my worst enemy. I didn't ruin your life' said a scared looking Sarah in a meek voice.

'I'm sorry Sarah I shouted. But the truth is Priya was far better. At least she left me alone' replied Aditya and without a backward glance walked to the train.

Sid shouted back 'Aditya! You are totally insane. Think about what you said just now!'

Aditya did not reply and didn't look once in their direction.

Sarah collapsed in a nearby bench. She was staring at the floor her eyes full of tears. Sid sat next to her and put an arm around her. The train began to move and she started to cry uncontrollably. Sid kept on patting her but she couldn't stop crying.

'Why do I still love him Sid bhaiya?'

'It's ok Sarah. He must've been under stress. He didn't seem to realize what he was talking. We'll talk it out soon' replied and began to try to calm down Sarah.

'No one has ever spoken to me like this. He... he hurt me. I never thought...this would happen' sobbed Sarah.

'We hurt the people we love the most Sarah. But what was that all about Priya? I'll see to it. He's going on like mad. I'll talk some sense into him.'

'No Sid. I'm not talking to him unless he realizes what the right thing is. There is no meaning in our love if he keeps on hurting me with his theories about Priya. I'm fed up with his Priya tales. I have feelings too. I'm not a coat hanger.'

And this was the beginning of Sarah's silent torture.

July
August
September
October…

The clock struck twelve
No sleep
One
Mind is buzzing
Two am
I felt like I lost someone
Cried myself out to sleep

You said you don't need me anymore
You don't like me
It hit me hard and that hurts!
I was a scared little kid
Who never wanted to get caught up in the mess!
You pulled me in
And now you cut me down.

The moment I thought everything is perfect
You cut in and said 'It's all over'
And when you left

The part of my heart
That was beating out for you
Bled so much
And I'm in pain.
And I feel so hollow.
I'm falling down like a wingless bird
Left alone in the cold!

*****

Chapter 13

Two days into Aditya's departure Sid called up and said he was going to Bangalore. He himself couldn't believe that he had made it to the Symbiosis University.

The sun was almost up in the sky. Its rays entered the windows of the bus and the gentle morning sun rays touched the soft cheek of Sarah who was sitting comfortably in the college bus near the window. She was seeing the shops on the road side moving away as the bus moved. Her iPod was singing the song 'When you are gone…' into her ears. When the bus crossed a Skoda car she was reminded of Aditya and it brought her flashes of his face in her mind. She couldn't find a single reason to hate him but she had a thousand reasons to like him.

She liked the way he walked and his cool attitude; he never feared anything or anyone, the way he spinned the basketball in his finger after his practice sessions, the way his hair looked after she had given it a ruffle, the way he sang and played his guitar (it makes her sit with her eyes glued to him), his smile that swept her off her feet, the way his eyes shone with affection when he looked into her eyes. No. It was never that all gooey look. 'Oh my God! How much I miss him!' thought Sarah and tears welled up in her eyes. Though she was looking outside, her thoughts were wandering around Aditya.

She turned to Preethi who was sitting beside her and said 'I don't know how I am gonna survive the next two years. I couldn't stay away from him without at least a phone call or a text for even two days at a stretch. But now, look.'

Preethi smiled understandingly at her and gave her hand a squeeze. Though she missed Aditya a lot she still felt the pain of their last encounter in the railway station and she was not ready to forgive him. He had called her up to say sorry. She refused to talk to him.

Though he had hurt her so badly, she prevented herself from hating him. 'There must be something wrong. He wouldn't have hurt me otherwise. But all this is not gonna convince me to talk to him' thought Sarah.

Aditya felt so miserable when she refused to talk to him even on the day he was about to leave for Australia. He apologized to Sid explaining that the conversation with his dad had made him go crazy and that he wanted to prove that he was capable of maintaining relationships.

'So you were ready to lose Sarah's love for your stupid challenge? That too for a moron like Priya?' asked Sid.

'I'm really sorry. She wouldn't talk to me now' said an upset Aditya.

'She's human Aditya. How do you expect her to be normal with you after all the mean stuff you told her?'

*****

As soon as Sarah reached home she found a parcel in the mail box. She was curious about it and she went to her room fast and began to open it carefully.

A maroon hard bound silver lettered book rolled out of the cover. The letters 'Pride and Prejudice' was embossed in the cover in silver. She was very much surprised to find it and when she opened the book a letter fell out of it.

She opened the letter and began reading it…

'Sarah!

Am gonna miss u. You are going away from me. Well… I'm going right?

Dunno how or when I'll be able to meet you.

This one's for you. Never written one for anybody, you are the first one.

As I see you moving away from me.....your image in my eyes blur.

I try hard to blink but it gets worse, my eyes are filled with tears, I dunno what to do!!

Am lost in a series of events running through my mind.

I can't forget my days with you. Now...so far away,

Dunno if my heart can take this blow,

You changed my world. You are the one who does understand me... but now you've left me for good in this darkness n' I shall perish in the dust.

You mean a lot to me.

My world will be away from me...so far away that each of us will be separated by busy hours, I'll have my work n' you'll have yours.

Soon the small castle of dreams that we built together will be torn apart n' we'll be busy building new ones...on our own, soon others will fill this void...that's left here...never in my life will I be able to understand why this was happening to me

Cuz I don't have the courage to believe in the assertiveness of our relationship!!

I'll be lost...soon somewhere...

I'll miss u a lot Sarah!!

I dunno n I fear what promises the future holds for us but for now... I'll be away from u!!

Into the dark shall I descend....take care of yourself. I won't be there to hold your hand anymore, but for one moment if I am with you, I'll hold you in my arms...weak as they are, but I'll keep you warm n safe, till I die!!.. Till my heart beats out to death cursing me why I had loved u...so much I made myself bleed to death!!

But I love u...

Always!!

Your love,

Aditya.

Sarah's eyes welled up with tears and she read and reread the letter. She closed her eyes and collapsed into a nearby chair. Her mind was on war as usual.

'Should I forgive Aditya?' thought Sarah.

The evil side of her mind said 'No Sarah. He hurt you. So take revenge.'

The angel side of her mind was like 'Of course Sarah! You should forgive him. What's the point in hurting the person you love?'

'No Sarah! Move on with your life'

The evening passed on slowly. Sarah couldn't concentrate.

*****

Chapter 14

College life turned into hell for Sarah. You can't expect any mercy from Sarah's psycho department staff. As soon as the semester had begun she had gotten into trouble with Ms. Ramani who handled 'Computer Networks'. Preethi often commented 'A lecturer with no intelligence at all is handling Networks'.

Ms. Ramani, a fat and gigantic looking lecturer who wore her old fashioned broad rimmed spectacles looked almost like a scary looking school teacher. Her English speaking skills had been so funny that Sarah and her bench mate Maya made it a habit to note it down whenever they found a new word to add to their vocabulary.

First day class…

'Good morning students! Computer Networks subject… I am going to handle of it.'

The class couldn't control its laughter. Sarah and Maya ducked down to hide their laughter. They looked around and found that almost everyone was sniggering. Ms. Ramani didn't find this behavior as amusing.

She called out 'Girls in the third bench! Please get up. Tell your joke to the whole class. We will also laugh of it. What are you mading(making) fun of?'

'Sorry mam' replied Sarah and Maya in unison.

'This is the first and last warning for you. Don't repeat of it. Okay?'

'Yes mam'

'Sit down. I know how to treat of people like you.'

'What language does she speak Sarah? Gibbonish?' murmured Maya.

'Heard she's so evil that she doesn't bother to fail students purposely' said Sarah.

'We hafta be careful then. We are already in her bad books' replied Maya.

*****

Aditya and Sarah had not spoken to each other in a really long time. Preethi and Sid once mentioned that he is seeing someone else.

Aditya tried to speak to Sarah and called her up but Sarah wouldn't talk to him. He got really worried and called up Preethi.

'Hey Preethi! How are you?'

'Aditya! What a surprise? What's up?' asked Preethi immediately.

'I have no idea. Sarah wouldn't just talk to me' said Aditya.

'She's going through hell because of you. Whatever it is Aditya, I hate to see my friend going through all the hardships like this. To make it even worse, you broke her heart. I'm not forgiving you for whatever you have done' said an angry Preethi.

'I know her much better than you do. She'll be fine.'

'You know nothing, Aditya. You don't deserve Sarah. You deserve only the dumbest females like Sanjana or Priya.'

'Just because she gets into trouble all the time doesn't mean I'm responsible, Preethi!' said Aditya.

'She doesn't keep getting into trouble, she chose trouble.'

'What do you want me to do? Make her stop loving me?'

'There are certain things that can't be undone Aditya! At least you could be grateful to her instead of being so cold but you broke her heart!'

'Bye Preethi!' said Aditya.

And the line went dead. Preethi though funny was not dumb. So she didn't tell Sarah anything regarding this phone call. She was so angry that she called up Sid and yelled at him.

'Sid! I would never have been friends with even you if I had known Aditya was so mean' shouted Preethi into her phone. She was almost in tears. She had had enough with Sarah being so indifferent these days.

'Hey Preethi! Stop crying now. What's wrong?' asked Sid.

'Ask me what is correct, Sid? Nothing is normal around here lately ever since we heard Aditya is moving on. Sarah's gone almost mad. She already had problems with the lecturers in her department. She got into trouble with Ms. Ramani. You know that female, right? She failed Sarah purposely twice and now her internal marks have gone really low. And Prof. Rajan… he's torturing her like mad. She's standing out of his class most of the time' cried Preethi.

'Is that all? You scared me. But how come she got into trouble with postcard (Prof.Rajan)?' asked Sid with a laugh.

'Don't laugh Sid. It's all because of you and Aditya. He keeps smiling maliciously and passing over snide comments about us all. He keeps telling her that 'Certain people don't come to college for studying, do they Sarah?' or 'People from popular gangs will be treated in a different way. They will actually be spending most of their precious time out of my class.' He asks questions for which no one in the class has found answers and he sends her out of the class in every possible chance. And now to make it worse Aditya has left her. She's gotten into postcard's bad books all because of Aditya and now look…'

'Sorry Preethi! This is all because of us. He never really liked Aditya and me. Particularly Aditya. I never thought Postcard will react in this way. How is Sarah now?'

'She's mad. She doesn't speak to me anymore. She pretends in front of my mom but it's horrible to see her like this. She's not her usual self. No expression at all... you should've seen her. She looks like a zombie. Scary it is. I found her crying into her pillow one day. And I read her diary yesterday. Pathetic! She wants to talk only to you but she doesn't want to disturb you either. Since her ego doesn't let her be she wouldn't talk her heart out to me either. I dunno whether she sleeps at all. Her eyes are so red. And these professors take advantage of this situation when she's not speaking back to make her college life more miserable. To say in simple words, she's...lifeless. She'll listen only to you Sid. Please do something.'

'I'll talk to her! Now please you don't get frustrated. She'll need your help' replied Sid.

'Are you still the same old fool Sid?' asked Preethi to lighten the mood.

'I reckon you are still the same old monkey! I miss you guys a lot' said Sid.

'I miss you too!' replied Preethi.

*****

Sid called up Sarah.

'Hello' said a flat voice. Sid hadn't believed when Preethi told him about how Sarah was these days but her voice was of course lifeless.

'Sarah! Sid here. How are you?' asked Sid.

'Fine as usual. How are you?'

'Not as fine as you. Stop pretending and can you please tell me what's wrong with you?'

'Everything's fine Sid.'

'So?'

'So… I quit. I should've known. I didn't deserve him, Sid. It was because of me he broke up with Priya. So this has to happen to me.'

'Are you mad? What is this new theory that he broke up with Priya because of you? They broke up even before he knew you. You are so typically you Sarah. Always ready to own up other people's blame. Now he's just going out with Sanjana. He's not committed and he didn't break up with you either.'

'So are you asking me to wait for them to get committed and then become mad? Please Sid bhaiya. It's already hurting me a lot. Let me get over with this soon when he's still mine.'

'Don't you think you are doing the same mistake Aditya did with Priya?'

Sarah was silent.

'Aditya is not everything. Don't you think you are getting overly dependent on him? Why don't you live your life Sarah? Just think over what you said to Aditya the day you made him see some sense. And please for Preethi and my sake don't do anything foolish!' said Sid.

Sarah started sobbing into the phone. 'Don't worry Bhaiya! I won't kill myself because… I'm already dead.'

*****

Sarah thought 'I know he still loves me!'

During holidays she knew when Aditya was back in the country but she knew very well that he was in Mumbai.

Do you think it was easy for her to ignore him as if he was never a part of her life? No… Definitely not.

A sneak peek into her diary…

'Maybe I know why all this is happening to me. Maybe I was wrong all the time.

Aditya… I'm so sorry.

You've not actually left me. You've tried to teach me something that I would never have understood otherwise... Pain.

What does a painful heart mean?

I used to laugh when I read about somebody being heartbroken. Now I can feel the pain right here in my heart.

I always thought you were mad to feel so bad about your break up with Priya. No… I was mad to think that way.

I never really felt why you were so depressed when Priya left you but thanks to you. You have made me get the exact feelings that you once felt.

I have troubled you a lot to make you smile but I never knew how much it would have hurt you to smile. I can feel the pain now when I try to smile. Well… To get the exact meaning, I'll tell you. I've long forgotten what happiness is. And I've of course forgotten how to smile the smile you loved so much. What's the point in smiling when you are not around to give me your charming smile back? Am I not correct?

Preethi keeps telling that I don't even try to get over you. Maybe she's right. I don't want to lose you Aditya.

No one will understand it Aditya. I fell head over heels in love with you the moment I got to know you.

I was a dreamer. I loved you so much like the fairy tales I read and the days I spent with you were too good to be real. I don't want to give up those days. Those were the best part of my life that I chose for myself. I mean, it was the first best decision made by me in my life that was really going on successful until a few months back. I am not gonna blame anyone. It was fully my own decision. Maybe I was selfish to have wanted your love fully and still have a craving for it.

You told me how hollow you felt when Priya left. I feel the same hollowness without you Aditya. I'm dead already. I'm a mere corpse roaming about lifeless. I keep going because I don't want to hurt the others too like I've hurt you. I can   understand you well now. And I love you for all that you did for me. Even if you hadn't done anything I would have loved you all the same. So I'll just think that you never really entered my life. I'll do what I would've done when I came to know that you were committed to Priya already. But I couldn't block you out of my mind because whenever I was in trouble I used to think about you to ease up things and that behavior is quite hard to drop so suddenly. Because I'm getting into trouble so often these days that I've actually lost count. And you know what? I'm actually happy that these troubles find me since they keep me occupied for a while so that I can think about them rather than thinking about what went wrong between us. So like once you said, I'll need time too.

I'm sorry Aditya if I haven't given you all my love. I'm sure this girl will give you all her love that you deserve.

But Aditya… It hurts. Here in my heart. I can feel the pain surging through me. I'm alone in the dark. Please do come back. I'm not able to get over you. I need your love.

I can't ever hate you. I'll always love you!'

'I'm walking down the street
With only myself for company
It's not new to me
Cuz I'm used to being lonely.

Walking in the rain
All alone on a gloomy evening
With a broken heart
It was one such day that I met you.

I didn't know you would talk to me
Like a best friend who knew me for ages
You sailed into my life
As gently as you left me alone in the cold

You made me laugh
And dried my tears
Told me tales
And heard my dreams

So now you've left me
All alone in this dreary world

*I don't have anymore
Teardrops for you!'*

Teardrops fell down on her diary almost erasing what she had written as she closed her pen. She fell on her bed and closed her eyes to sleep where in her dreams she can escape the reality...the hard reality that Aditya had actually left her. She had trusted Aditya a lot. She had never loved (well... next to her mom) or trusted anyone in her life so much. She wasn't able to concentrate. So she took a week off and went to her home town.

Throughout her stay at home, she kept her croaky switched off which was an unusual behavior and she was in a really bad temper. She yelled at her little sister and everyone at home. She slapped her sister one day when she tried to play a prank on her. Her mom got really annoyed with her behavior and she shouted at Sarah 'What's wrong with you Sarah? You've never been like this before. Why did you hit her?'

Sarah got annoyed and shouted back 'I was wrong. I should have become a surgeon!'

She went to her room and showed her degree of anger by slamming the door tight shut with as much force as possible and remained shut in her room for the rest of the day. Her parents exchanged a look of disbelief of what was going on in front of their eyes.

The next day, Sarah was sitting in the porch of her house staring into the slow rain. Her mom brought her a steaming cup of coffee. Of course a lot can happen over a cup of coffee.

'Sarah! I know things are not like what they were used to be for you in college. I'm not pressing you to talk to me about it. But if you really want to speak out you can count on me' said Sarah's mom.

Sarah continued to sip her coffee. She didn't dare look up for she knew she would definitely cry.

After a minute's silence,

Sarah's mom came near her and gave her a hug and said 'Whatever is bothering you will get over soon. Don't worry!'

But this kindness was too much for Sarah to bear. She's definitely human. The emotions that she had kept suppressed in her already broken heart came up and she could feel the lump developing in her throat making it impossible for her to talk. Tears welled up in her eyes blurring her vision. And within five seconds she was crying badly in her mom's shoulders.

Mom- the only person who knows everything about you and still loves you. Sarah's mother was wonderful to whom she found herself narrating everything she had gone through all these days. Everything about her college and her friends and her love for Aditya came out in a flow and tears were streaming down her eyes as she started telling about Aditya. She didn't know what made her tell all these stuff to her mom but she felt quite free in her heart after her confession.

'I am disappointed Sarah! Not because you loved someone but you hid this from me for two years' said Sarah's mother.

'I couldn't bring myself to... I was scared you would shout at me and disown me for good. I am sorry. It all seems so absurd when I think about it now. How could I have gone through all this, ma? ' replied Sarah.

Silence...

Sarah's mum went on...

'What's the purpose of your life, Sarah? Did I send you to college to find the love of your life? Life is not a fairytale where there is always a Prince Charming and the Princess and finally they lived happily ever after. Come to reality.'

'I am not saying that love is wrong and I am not opposing your love for that guy Aditya. But everything has got its own time. You are just nineteen. I thought you had brains enough to understand that fact. You are really good in advising others but when it comes to you, you forget the fact that your advice applies to you too. Don't be a hypocrite. Think what you really want now. Other things can wait. There's still more time for you to fall in love' and added 'One more thing Sarah, it's never a mistake to shower your love upon a person but it goes terribly awful when the chosen person is wrong. I'm not threatening you. I just ask you to be careful in everything you do. Because I really love you and care for you Sarah.'

Saying this she left Sarah alone to think on her own.

'Love you too mom' whispered Sarah.

*****

That night Sarah couldn't sleep. Her mother's words echoed in the walls of her mind.

Sarah thought-

'Yes. Mum's correct. I really do have time…for everything.'

For the first time in weeks she had succeeded in keeping Aditya out of her thoughts. Finally she fell asleep and had a dreamless sleep first time in about four months.

Before Sarah left for college again her mum told her in the railway station 'Sarah dear! You have always been a good girl and you still are. You always have our love and support. You will make us proud of you one day' and gave her a hug. Sarah controlled her tears and got into the train. She felt like a first year crying with all the people watching. She hated crying in public but she couldn't help it now. She waved bye to her mum and dad until they disappeared from view.

Chapter 15

For the next few months Sarah worked a lot. She had time only for herself. And by the end of final year her team's project won them grand prize money. Ms.Ramani was smug about their success. Nothing that she did would deter Sarah now. It was just a beginning. She wanted to make it big. She wanted to land herself in a job with 'Facebook', her dream.

Final year and final semester approached fast.

The campus placement season…

Sarah was confident that she would make her dream come true. But her luck had it otherwise.

The list of students who made it to the second round of selection was displayed in the bulletin board. Sarah went to check when the second round was and she had the worst shock in her life. Her name was not in the list.

'Hey Sarah! It was that Ramani who was in charge of displaying the results' said Veena to Sarah.

Sarah went in search of Ms. Ramani to the staff room. There she was chatting merrily with her colleague. Sarah approached her in the most polite way she could ever imagine for this cold hearted female, 'Excuse me madam!'

Prof. Ramani looked up through her spectacles which were halfway down her nose giving her an old librarian kind of look. 'Oh! Sarah! What brings you here?' asked the professor.

'Mam, I think there's a mistake in the selection results' replied Sarah.

'That is absolutely not possible Sarah!'

'Can you please check it once, mam? I'm sure I would have got through the first round.'

'Oh! So…your name is not there. It means you are not selected. Don't be over confident of it.'

Even under this stressful situation Sarah couldn't help but notice Prof.Ramani's unnecessary usage of 'of it' in her sentences which made her almost laugh.

'Mam, can you please just check once?'

'I'm very busy now Sarah! I'll check of it when I'm free.'

Sarah was cursing her in her mind 'Traitor!'

She didn't thank her and returned to her class where everyone who got selected was talking excitedly about the second round that afternoon.

'Afternoon? This afternoon! The second round is today?' screamed Sarah.

'Yes. Why?' asked Veena.

'That stupid thing refused to check the list immediately saying that she's busy' replied Sarah.

That afternoon…

Sarah was sitting in the almost empty classroom. She was thinking about how her entire dream has become a nightmare in just minutes.

Prof. Rajan entered the classroom asking for his lost book. 'Oh no! Not him now. Please let postcard not see me!' prayed Sarah.

But Sarah's prayer went in vain. He found Sarah and exclaimed 'You are here! Isn't the second round of recruitment going on?'

'Yes sir' replied Sarah who was not in a mood to become an object of ridicule at this instance.

'Why didn't you go?'

'Actually, my name is not listed' replied Sarah with acid in her tone.

'What? That's so not possible. A student with academic excellence like you… There must be some mistake' wondered Prof. Rajan.

Sarah couldn't believe her ears. Was it really postcard giving her a compliment?

'Go straight to the seminar hall. I'll see what went wrong' said the Professor.

Sarah was standing as if rooted to the floor. She couldn't believe what was happening. Postcard… Sorry! Professor Rajan was actually helping her.

'Go now! What are you waiting for?' asked Professor that woke her to her senses.

She grabbed her bag and after uttering a quick 'Thank you sir!' ran to the seminar hall. After a long time she experienced happiness in her life.

Sarah can already feel it in her heart that she had succeeded as she sped to the seminar hall. She was actually smiling and felt very much full of life.

*****

After two long hours…

Sarah was sitting in the cafeteria waiting for Preethi. She started scribbling a song in her diary.

> *'A little class*
> *Big windows*
> *A windy day*
>
> *Lots of notes*
> *Long lectures*
> *Maya's sleeping*
> *Wat do I do?*
>
> *I look around*
> *And caught his eye*
> *Was he looking at me?*
>
> *Is it real?*
> *Is it true?*
> *Must be a dream*
>
> *Years later…*
> *A summer sky*
> *An empty class*
> *Standing in the middle of the benches*
> *I can feel the days we spent together*
> *Days of joy n' fun*

No more sleepy lectures
No more internal mark threats
And no more little fights
And no more happy endings
No more Prince Charming
And no more fairy tales

I never wanted this abrupt end
And never did you
Now tell me
Wat do I do?'

After almost an eon later Preethi came almost dancing with joy. As soon as she caught a glimpse of Sarah she screamed 'Sarah, my love! I did it! Got into TCS. Can't wait to tell this to Sid and my brother! They won't believe a word I say.'

She added after a moment's thought 'Oops! I heard Ramani's conspiracy against you. I'm sorry' said Preethi sadly.

'You need not try to act sad Preethi. I got the internship' said Sarah calmly.

'Oh My God! Really! Congrats!' screamed Preethi in joy.

'If it hadn't been for Prof.Rajan's timely intervention, Ramani would have succeeded in ruining my life' said Sarah.

'Professor Rajan? The postcard? I thought he hated you' said Preethi a bit puzzled.

'I dunno. Even I'm confused. But seriously he's not the same old postcard anymore. I have some respect for him. Maybe he was trying to help me all this time!' replied Sarah and narrated the entire tale to Preethi.

After a while, Sarah was smiling to herself.

'Did you actually smile now?' asked a surprised Preethi and pulled her note and took a look at it.

'Wow! That's nice! Now that you have everything you want, you can ask Arjun out on a date, can't you?' Preethi winked.

When Preethi told Sid about the placement results he was overwhelmed. He told Sarah 'Good for you girl! I always knew you will do it! Finally you got your attitude back!'

As for Sarah's parents, they were in cloud nine. After all, their daughter has proved herself in spite of all the obstacles. They were happier than Sarah and they were happy for her.

*****

Chapter 16

Preethi entered the room to find Sarah lying on the bed. She was seeing the photos on the digital photo frame. She stopped on seeing the photo the four of them had taken together during Sid's birthday party in his house.

'Do you still love him?' asked Preethi.

'Actually I'm taking a look at your digital photo frame and not the photo. I love technology!' replied Sarah.

'I asked you something' said Preethi further pressing into the matter.

'What is love?' retorted Sarah.

'As you very well know I hate riddles, Sarah!'

'Well… I love them.'

'Fine. My dear sphinx, I accept defeat. So how was Delhi?'

'Delhi was the usual. I had nightmares again. Chased me out from there.'

'How was your meeting with the psychiatrist?'

'Well. He said I am perfectly normal. It's only up to me to stop imagining stuff. He said that I have got to stop blaming myself for everything that goes wrong around me. He asked me to take a break and so I did' replied Sarah in a somewhat cheerful tone.

'Well... Why don't you stop imagining stuff then?'

'I don't imagine idiot! Thoughts just keep rushing. I couldn't control them. You know what? I just feel like I want to yell all these stuff at him once. A last chance is what I need and then I will be fine. Otherwise it's like I feel like I have been cheated out for good. I want to tell him that he was the one who broke the trust and that he is so mean and that he screwed up my life' said Sarah earnestly.

'You'll have your day. Patience, Sarah! Before that we need to get some fresh air. We girls need to go out for a while. We need to do our graduation shopping remember?' said Preethi.

'Perfect! I wanna go shopping! It'll keep me occupied' thought Sarah.

*****

Chapter 17

It was the old coffee shop - the good old cafe where the four had hung around during their college days, the place that had felt their presence, and the shop which had missed them for the past two years. Sarah was sitting in the same old table facing the garden. Well… She was not alone. Preethi accompanied her and they were both waiting for Sid.

It began to rain outside and the evening turned gloomy. The lane was already empty. Sarah was looking at the cars that were parked nearby thinking about the Skoda that Aditya once owned. 'Will he still own the Skoda? No… He would have bought some better car' thought Sarah.

Sarah's cappuccino came and she was sipping it slowly and the warmth began to spread through her veins. She was still reminiscing the moments she had shared with Aditya. The Taylor Swift song 'Breathe' was playing in the background. Perfect song at the right moment.

'Time seemed to fly when he was with me. I felt so free and least bothered about everything. No nightmares. No fear. No tears as I had his love to get me going' thought Sarah. 'Well... It was my past. Aditya was my past. He won't come back into my life and I don't want him to come back either.'

Every little memory of Aditya flashed in front of her eyes. She still remembered the day he proposed his love and how gently he kissed her fingers. She could still feel the firmness with which he would hold her hand. She felt as if everything had happened only yesterday.

How many plans?

Plans of future...of love and happiness. He had always listened to her silly talks like how she liked pirates when she was a small girl after reading 'The Treasure Island'. She used to sing the song 'Yoho...' and he would say 'I should never have taken you to that pirate movie.'

She would reply 'You can do anything but you can't take the pirate out of Cap'n Jack Sparrow.'

'Oh shut up silly!' he used to say.

Now Sarah thought 'How nice it would have been if we hadn't had that break up. We were both madly in love...once. Did he really love me?'

'Oh shut the crap!' thought Sarah and tried to block her thoughts about Aditya.

Suddenly something soft tapped against her cheek. She had been so deeply engrossed in her thoughts that she hadn't noticed the black Skoda that drove in, hadn't heard the bell ring and hadn't noticed the tall figure walking towards her. There he was Aditya- the one and only Aditya who Sarah knew and would ever know standing in front of her. He kissed her cheek and held out a red rose saying 'Hi love!' and pulled a chair to sit beside her. She was shocked on seeing Aditya.

'What the hell is he doing here? How dare he kiss me?' she thought as she took the rose and looked at him like seeing an alien.

But deep within her heart, on seeing him she immediately felt like the same old first year girl who had run behind him admiring whatever he did. She forgot all the stuff she had to yell at him that she had rehearsed in her head for ages. No way! She was happy that right before her eyes was Aditya, the person whom she had loved once… and forever. She was resisting the urge to run into his arms and hold on to him tightly.

When Sarah finally got rid of the voices in her head, she murmured in a surprised voice 'Aditya?'

'Yeah, it's me' he smiled.

'So… How's life?' stammered Sarah.

'Going on great. You can see me' replied Aditya with a smile that lit his face.

Aditya saw Sarah's eyes that were as usually been neatly lined with an eye liner but it was quite thicker than usual. It made her look even more beautiful.

'Congrats! I heard you are going to the US' said Aditya.

'Yep! Thanks.'

Aditya's espresso came. He always liked espresso. Sarah used to look at his espresso like something disgusting but today she eyed it quite normally as she had gotten used to it.

Aditya was gazing at Sarah and Sarah felt her cheeks burning.

She said 'Stop staring at me, Aditya!'

'Oh sorry! I can't help it. I have almost forgotten how beautiful you look!' replied Aditya.

A few seconds passed by. Preethi who was sitting next to Sarah got restless. 'What the hell are they doing? Socializing or what?' thought Preethi.

After a minute or so Aditya began, 'Actually Sarah I need to talk to you about something really important.'

'Well... I'm not a saint, Aditya. I'm very much human' replied Sarah curtly.

She could feel the love leaving the air. The imaginary hearts circling their heads all this while went out with a pop. Everything seemed cold. 'At last' thought Preethi.

'Sarah! Please listen to me. You don't seem to understand. Two years without you was really hard for me too. I missed you a lot and when you finally chose to ignore me I was totally helpless. It was at this point I decided...'

Sarah cut in '...you decided to get rid of me and get yourself a new girlfriend. Enough of all this drama.'

'What?' asked Aditya.

'Stop it Aditya!' shouted Sarah. The entire coffee shop went silent. 'I have had enough of you and your theories. I came here... to finally let go of the memories and not to listen to anymore stories about your life and your ex girlfriends or the recent ones and I'm telling you I am leaving you forever. Forever I say. You don't have any idea what I went through the past two years. You broke my heart. You don't give a damn about me for two years and come back one day to finally tell me that you are in love with someone else. I am mad to have trusted you. I should have realized that you are just another rich guy who keeps changing girlfriends like cars. Damn! I will not regret this Aditya. I know where my love stands. I admired you and everything you did. I admired your love Aditya! My love is true. Even now I'm struggling to find words to hurt you. I need to hurt you Aditya to let you know how badly you have hurt me. But I can't hurt you Aditya because I've never stopped loving you. Please leave' said Sarah and tears started to blind her. She couldn't control herself from crying now that the tears have escaped her eyes.

Aditya got up, walked towards Sarah and held her shoulders firmly. 'Look here Sarah!' She avoided looking at him. So he held her face up and wiped her tears gently and said 'Sarah! I'm sorry I hurt you badly but that was not my intention.'

'It went totally berserk. I was upset the day I left. I wanted to prove to my Dad that my love for you is true. I shouldn't have yelled at you. And then after reaching Australia, I got this cool idea that if you started to believe that I have moved on you will work hard to forget me. I know revenge makes you work better than love. I know you would do anything to keep me off your mind and start living your normal life the way you would have if you had never met me. And that was what I needed. But I'm really sorry Sarah! I know I've hurt you so much. I never thought you would love me so much that even now I know you will forgive me' smiled Aditya stroking her cheek.

Sarah blankly looked at him tears streaming down her cheeks.

'Look outside' said Aditya pointing to a car. Sarah looked out and saw the shiny black Skoda. 'My car's still with me and so is my girlfriend, both too good to lose' smiled Aditya.

Aditya knelt down and took Sarah's hands in his and said 'I love you Sarah! You are the one who made me go on. You taught me to live. And you know what, Sarah. Till this moment, everything I do, I do it for you.'

He kissed her fingers.

Sarah looked into his eyes wondering whether it was true or was it gonna be just another dream.

Aditya reached for his pocket and took out a tiny box. He opened it and took out a pretty ring. He fixed his gaze with hers and said 'If I don't ask you now, someone else surely will because you are prettier than you were before. My dearest Sarah! I know I can't live without you. I want to spend the rest of my life with you. Will you marry me?'

Sarah was dazed by these sudden turn of events. This is the second time in her life Aditya had made her go dumb. She couldn't think. She looked at Preethi who was smiling now.

All of a sudden Sid entered, 'Am I late?' asked Sid loudly.

Sarah suddenly understood that it had been planned by everyone as usual. He hadn't left her after all. And he never will.

She looked into Aditya's eyes and whispered 'One condition if I have to say yes'.

'What's that?' asked Aditya.

'You have to wait till I'm ready. I'm going to study MS. I've got a scholarship' replied Sarah.

'I respect your decision. I'll wait for you my entire life, Sarah. Now can I have your word please, senorita?' he asked with a mocking courtesy.

'Well… yes' said Sarah with a wide smile.

Aditya smiled and wore the ring on her finger. Sarah was staring unbelievably at him. He said 'Trust me. I love you!' and hugged her. Sid and Preethi clapped for their friends and were soon joined by the people in the coffee shop who had been seeing all these proceedings with their mouths open.

'Is this some Bollywood movie?' someone commented.

Stupidity unplugged, yet again!

*****

Epilogue

I t was the first day of November.
All Soul's Day.

The day had been unusually bright for a November day and the sky was clear. There were no symptoms of storm. The evening sun which looked like it was about to disappear beneath the ocean spread its golden orangy glow across the horizon.

As the time passed by cool sea breeze started to blow towards the shore.

It was a full moon night and so the night too was bright. The waves were quite high. The beach was calm except for the sound of the sea.

As the moon shone upon the beach with its shy smile, a young couple was walking slowly on the sand keeping a pretty good distance from the water. The young man put his arm around his love and held her close to him.

'I feel like playing in the water!' said Sarah.

'No... Not today. The tide is really high' replied Aditya and increased his grip on her scared that she would run straight to the water.

Sarah just smiled and placed her head on the chest of her over protective lover as they stood watching the lovely tide.

Aditya held her close and said 'I love you Sarah... more than life.' He took a deep breath and said 'Every time I see you, I fall in love with you all over again.'

No words were spoken after that. Silence said it all.

******